drama diaries

unscripted

by Lainey McBride

by Betsy Howie
Illustrated by Mike Lowery

SCHOLASTIC INC.

For Chuck,
Mary Lou,
Tim and
Randy

ISBN 978-0-545-39705-6

Text copyright © 2012 by Betsy Howie.
Cover art by Allison Cole.
Interior art by Mike Lowery.
Photo credits: Girl on cover © Paul Costello/Getty Images;
shoes © Zoonar/Thinkstock; notebook paper © Roel Smart/iStockphoto;
paper © lumpynoodles/iStockphoto;
Al Jolson © Corbis, courtesy of Betsy Howie.

12 11 10 9 8 7 6 5 4 3 2 1   12 13 14 15 16 17/0

Printed in the U.S.A.   40
First Scholastic printing, November 2012
Book design by Jennifer Rinaldi Windau

LLMF

Dear Writer/Researcher/Fan,

Welcome to the Legendary Lainey McBride Foundation! We appreciate your interest in this extraordinarily gifted actress and all-around fabulous entertainer.

You may think of this as an archive where every important thought, conversation, and keepsake that involves Lainey McBride is kept— it's sort of like a diary, but more important and official. This archive has been put together by Lainey McBride herself. She began her archival work at the age of twelve as a courtesy to her future biographers and fans (you). Ms. McBride regrets having not started sooner, but attempts to recapture her early years through storytelling, photographs, and mementos. She hopes you forgive her for the delay.

We are glad you're here!

Sincerely,

The Legendary Lainey McBride Foundation

12 YEARS 1 MONTH 15 DAYS

My name is Lainey McBride. I am twelve. I am not famous. But that is because I am twelve and I am starting from scratch since my parents aren't famous either. (Strictly speaking, I understand that's not the *only* way to get famous at twelve, but you don't have to read very many *People* magazines to figure out it's one of the *best* ways.)

But that is not what we're here to discuss.

This is what we're here to discuss: I have this feeling that my career is about to really take off and there's going to be lots of stuff to document, which is why this archive is so important. All those one-of-a-kind rare notes and documents have to go somewhere so they are safe in the years and decades to come.

You see, I have a big audition at the end of next month. I'm auditioning to be Anne in *The Diary of Anne Frank* at the Kokomo Players. But this is not just any production of *Anne Frank*. This production is going to be directed by Rodney Vaccaro. I don't know if you know who Rodney Vaccaro is, so I will tell you. He is a very important director from Indianapolis and he has NEVER directed at Kokomo before. This is a seriously large deal for Kokomo and, of course, for the actress who gets cast as Anne Frank. You may not realize it but sometimes big-time movies get shot in Indianapolis, and when they do, they sometimes cast people from Indiana in some of the parts.

I'll give you one guess who always ends up helping to cast the Indiana people.

Yup.

Rodney Vaccaro!

Once Rodney knows who you are, you are in very good shape from an Indiana point of view. You know what they say about show business—it's not what you know, it's *who* you know!

Right now, I don't really know much of anybody.

Well, that's not true really. I mean, I know some really great people, like Tammy (my best friend). She's the *best* best friend you could ever ask for. Not that she has connections in show business—she's not that kind of "who" . . . as in, it's *who* you know. You know? But she does always know just what to say, and what Tammy says about being from Fairmount, Indiana, is this: "Everybody has to start somewhere."

Now, back to the archives. Archives are important. I have read a lot of biographies (mostly about Maeve Winkley, the most amazing and versatile stage and film star currently living) and it always seems like there's so much left out about famous people's childhoods. I guess no one was looking carefully enough because no one knew it was going to be important someday. They missed the chance to get a glimpse at the road map that leads to extraordinary.

Even I don't know exactly how I'm supposed to get there, yet. But I'll figure it out. And I'll record it in here, so that when people tell my story they'll be able to do it right . . . with as much detail as possible. They will truly know *Lainey McBride, PFP (Pre-Famous Person)*.

They will know how much I wanted to fulfill my potential amazing-ness. They will understand what I did and what I gave up and how hard I worked (and even how much it hurt sometimes when it seemed like maybe my amazing-ness was never going to get its chance to show through to the outside world).

POSSIBLE BACK-OF-BOOK QUOTE
FOR ANY LAINEY BIO:

Any kid who reads (INSERT YOUR LAINEY BIO TITLE HERE) will know for certain they're not the only one who ever started from nowhere with a dream of getting somewhere and didn't know how they would but then somehow they did.

A few notes before we get going. First, I'm going to have my archives with me at all times so that I can write some things down as they're happening. Also, I'm not going to date my entries. I'm okay right now with people knowing how old I am. I mean, I'm sort of okay about it. Okay. I'm nervous. I'm nervous about turning thirteen because it's become really clear to me that if you turn thirteen before you get your first break you have almost no hope of ever becoming a child star. So, basically, I have 318 days left if I am going to reach stardom while I'm still a child.

That's extremely nerve-racking.

Now, I don't *have* to become a child star to fulfill my dreams, but I think it would be cool. I guess I just like the sound of it. *Child star.* Makes it sound like the person has so much greatness inside of them that said greatness can't wait till the person is eighteen to come out. And don't worry. I know it's tricky to be a child star and avoid getting spoiled and involved in delinquent behavior but

I also know it's tricky to be unknown in Fairmount. Personally, I think I could handle it. I think I could be famous on Broadway and in Hollywood without making bad choices because I've had a solid un-famous beginning here in Fairmount. But like I said to Tammy on the bus this morning, "There's nothing harder than being someone nobody has heard of, in a town nobody has heard of, in a state nobody ever considers when making vacation plans. That's the hardest thing in the world."

Tammy gave me the look that means "I have no idea what you just said but even so, I think you might not be quite right." What she actually said was "My cousins from Michigan vacation here every summer."

Tammy is very talented at agreeing with people without losing her point. I'm very not. That's why we decided last year that besides being my assistant, she should also be my spokesperson. The rule is, if I hear Tammy start to say, "What Lainey means to say is . . ." I'm supposed to stop talking. No matter what.

Tammy is also a total genius at Celebrity Sculpey. She can make a Sculpey version of absolutely any famous person you can name. Here is a picture of Sculpey Jeanne Heaton. (Let me just say right here, I think Jeanne is a fine dramatic actress even if she is ridiculously thin.)

I put up a special ledge in my bedroom that goes all the way around the room just so Tammy's Sculpey genius gets the attention it deserves.

Jeanne
Heaton

IMPORTANT LAINEY MCBRIDE LIFE PHILOSOPHY:
People should get the attention they deserve.

I like doing Sculpey figures, too. But I'm not as talented at it as Tammy is. And plus, I only do Maeve Winkley. I've done twenty-seven Maeves so far and they all go on a separate Maeve shelf in my room. Every time I find a picture of her in a new gown, I make a new Maeve.

I guess it's time to give you a little information about the other people who live in my house.

Mom works at Fair Flowers. Anybody who gets married in Fairmount gets their arrangements from Fair Flowers. I think she's secretly glad I'm going to be famous. She can't admit it because that would be like disagreeing with Dad, but sometimes when I talk about my plans, I see something light up in her eyes. She's got pretty, dark eyes (like her hair) and they don't usually look too lit up, so when it happens you notice. It happened the other day when she said she'd take off work two weeks from Saturday to drive me over to Kokomo for that audition I mentioned.

This is Maeve from the Academy Awards this year.

A florist mom isn't as helpful to my career as a famous mom or an agent mom would be. No doubt. But she'll be able to make arrangements for my dressing rooms and opening nights and premieres. I'm glad she'll be able to be my personal florist, because I don't want to feel like I'm leaving her behind.

It's trickier with my dad. His eyes never light up when it comes to my acting career. (Though I have to admit, he has the most amazing blue eyes. I wish I had inherited them. I got my blond hair from him but I got my mom's brown eyes.)

Anyways. He used to be in the army. I mean, technically speaking, I guess he still is in the army except it's been about four years since he got this temporary discharge thing-ee because of injuring his back and hip in some kind of drill, which is just an army way of saying *rehearsal*. (He was rehearsing being in a war zone, which, by the way, the army calls a theatre. How's that for wacky?)

Anyway, his hip and back made it impossible for him to be in the army for real after that injury. Although between you, me, and the lamppost (as Nana would say), I wouldn't ever say that to him, because if he heard me say he wasn't in the army "for real," it would turn into a very bad day for me.

Anyway, now he walks with a limp but he says it's getting better and that he'll be going back to the army when it's healed. While he's waiting, he spends most of his time out in the garage fixing engines and motors that people bring over. That's the kind of stuff he did in the army and he doesn't want to forget what he knows.

OFF THE RECORD:
I don't know if my dad really is getting better or not but I'm pretty sure he doesn't get to stay on that temporary thing-ee forever. I happened to overhear my mom on the phone with her sister saying, "Sooner or later, they're going to kick him out for good." That's going to be a bad day for everybody.

Honestly, I don't know what he's going to do if he does get kicked out for good. Even though we never talk to each other and we don't understand each other and I wonder if it's possible that we don't really even like each other, I feel kinda bad for him sometimes. I think it's possible that he needs the army like I need to be a famous actress. Maybe that's why he's so angry at me all the time.

I still have a shot at my dreams and he doesn't.

I wish I could think of some way that he could be a part of my rise to fame, because I know he really does love me deep down. Every once in a while, he shows up at the doorway of my room and looks like he's going to say something that has something to do with my life. Like, something that would really help us bond. But then he sees all the Sculpeys and the *People* magazine covers I use for wallpaper and no matter what else he might have come to say, this is what he actually says: "You just can't get enough. Can you?" (Like there's something wrong with that.) I just say no, and then we're kinda back to being strangers again. But after he leaves, I always wonder what it was he thought he was going to say before he got so distracted by Tammy's Sculpeys and my wallpaper.

Anyway, moving on . . . next is Chip, my brother. He's a year older than me but you'd never know it because he's littler than me, and he has dark hair. Plus, he creeps around like he wants to be invisible.

Basically, the only time you really know he's around is when he's blowing his trombone *really* loud in the room *right next to mine* while I am rehearsing. Our bedrooms share a wall. This is unfortunate.

Bottom line? The only person in my whole family who truly understands me is Nana Cake.

I know. It sounds weird, but it really is her last name. She was married to a McBride when dad was born, but then took back her maiden name when they got divorced. No wonder I'm "pleasingly plump." My relatives are named after desserts.

Anyway, Nana is my biggest fan and she understands exactly what it's like to have something special burning inside. Nana wanted to be an actress when she was young but her family said it wasn't

7

proper, and so she ended up marrying Frank McBride and that was that.

"It's a shame to be fifty before you explore what's truly special inside you," she said to me once. (That's how old she was when she finally auditioned for a play for the first time.) "You have to follow your passion from the start, Lainey, or there's no point in anything."

Whenever I'm in a play, she sends me flowers and a card that says "You Shine!"

And whenever she's in a play at the Double-A Community Players up in Ann Arbor, Michigan, where she lives, I send her a card that says "You Shine More!"

Moving on. My favorite teacher is Mrs. Davies. She does not really understand what it is to be an artist but she does take me seriously.

Last week after English, when Tammy and I told her I was auditioning for *Anne Frank,* she said, "Lainey. You don't really look like Anne Frank. Anne Frank had dark hair and was . . . well, quite thin."

I'm blond and . . . well, quite *not*.

This is where it gets clear that Mrs. Davies is not an artist in her soul. I like Mrs. Davies a lot. She has really helped me figure out diagramming sentences and I don't think just any teacher could do that and she doesn't treat me like I'm a kid most of the time. But she doesn't understand that an actress truly changes when she's acting.

I was just about to tell Mrs. Davies that she doesn't understand what it's like to be an artist when Tammy said: "What Lainey means to say is"—(Cue LAINEY to stop talking!)—"she appreciates your suggestions."

Mrs. Davies smiled. Tammy's really good at what she does.

Last year, when I did all my own talking, Mrs. Davies never smiled.

But honestly! It's not about looks. It's about what's inside. I can find the heart and soul of Anne Frank. If I do my job, I will become Anne Frank and the audience will see her in me, too. Nana Cake talks about finding character from the inside out all the time. And when I took an acting class with Madame Ava Foster in Fort Wayne last year, she said, "Dahling, your audience will see the character you show them!"

Tammy and I are going to go to the library tomorrow to check out the script for *The Diary of Anne Frank*. I have to start studying the script and researching the role. It's a lot of work to prepare for an audition.

I think that's pretty much all you need to know. Besides, I have to go to bed. I have school in the morning.

Oh! One last thing. My resume:

Lainey McBride

ACTRESS/SINGER/DANCER (AKA TRIPLE THREAT)
AGENT: CATHERINE CAKE, 232-555-4493

THEATRE:
The Music Man / Kokomo Players / Girl in Town
Bolts & Nuts / Fairmount Middle School / Lutie Spinks
The Wizard of Oz / Fairmount Civic Theatre / Apple Tree
Pinocchio / Marion Children's Theatre / Mrs. Bonaventura

TELEVISION:
Merry Christmas, Kokomo! / WKOK-TV, Channel 5 / Singer
Jerry's Home Furnishing / Labor Day Sale Ad / Girl in Chair

TRAINING AND EDUCATION:
Tap, Jazz, Ballet: Miss Margy's Dance School
Singing: Mr. Christianson, Fairmount Middle School
Acting Lessons: Madame Ava Foster, Fort Wayne Players

SPECIAL SKILLS:
Can sing louder than a trombone

You can see now how perfect it would be if I got the role of Anne Frank.

I've done the Midwestern townsperson (*The Music Man*). I've done the English Cockney maid (*Bolts & Nuts*). Imagine if I could add Anne Frank to the list. It would really prove I have the range of a great actress.

It's still the same day. I'm still the same age. It's 11:47 P.M. and I can't sleep, so I went downstairs to get something to eat but I couldn't get into the kitchen because Mom is still up. She's out on the back porch smoking. Dad is in the family room watching an old movie about Russian spies. My parents don't usually talk to each other very much. But when they're not doing it late at night and sitting in different rooms, it usually means they're not talking about something specific.

There are three rules in my family I didn't mention earlier:

1. Never say "Thank you" when someone buys you dinner. Say "I had a lovely time." Dad says if you thank them for the dinner, then you might as well say, "Thanks for the food I just chewed up and am now digesting." Dad says that's rude. It's much more appropriate to thank the person for the time they spent with you and the experience you had and not for the food they bought you. I know. It's weird.

2. Always say "McBride Residence" when you answer the phone. You never know when it might be a military situation and there's no time to waste making sure you're talking to the right person!

3. Never talk about Marty.

12 YEARS 1 MONTH 16 DAYS

So today started out pretty normally. Chip and I waited for the bus. I talked to the Wood girls. Chip talked to no one. I sang along to every single song on the bus radio. Chip plugged his ears. Like I said, pretty standard stuff. But then I got off the bus, and the next thing I know, Tammy is coming at me at 179 miles an hour!

She was totally out of breath, so it was kind of hard to understand her, but this is about what she said.

"Susan Sanchez told me that Michaela Bradshaw told her that Heidi Stewart heard that Libby Chamber is trying out for *The Diary of Anne Frank*!"

Then she just stopped talking and stared at me like I was going to have some fainting spell or something. But I played it totally cool.

"Figures," I said, and I threw my backpack on my back and started walking toward school.

"But she is so *not* Anne Frank, Lainey! That part belongs to you!" Tammy seemed really mad, which is unusual for her.

"Does she know I'm trying out?" I asked her.

"Yup." Tammy nodded like it was the worst news in the world.

"And how does she know?" I stopped and looked her in the eye.

"Ummmm," Tammy stuttered, "I don't know. Probably Susan told Michaela and Michaela told Heidi—"

"Just tell me what she said," I asked.

Tammy hesitated, but then she told me exactly what I needed to hear.

TAMMY
She said there was no way you'd ever get cast as Anne Frank, because you've got the wrong hair and . . . you're the wrong size.

"Why are you smiling, Lainey?" Tammy was shocked at my reaction. "Not only is she trying to get your part but she's being really mean."

We were in the hallway now and about to be late for class. I didn't have a lot of time to explain, but I tried my best.

"It's a sign, Tammy!" I whispered, as we walk-don't-run down the hall.

"But you said signs were good things that made you sure you were on the right track!" she whispered back.

"Exactly!" I answered. "The fact that Libby, who lives all the way over in Kokomo, cares enough to find out whether I, Lainey McBride, am auditioning is a sign! And the fact that she felt like she had to be mean about it is another sign!"

"I don't get it," Tammy said, standing in front of her homeroom. I turned to her and smiled.

> A NOTE
> ABOUT DIALOGUE:
> I am going to write really important conversations in script form. This will help screenwriters turn my story into a biopic (showbiz lingo for a movie that's a biography). My story is to be told on the silver screen with complete accuracy!

Libby Chamber is afraid of auditioning against Lainey McBride. And that, my dear Tammy, means that I have finally developed a reputation that precedes me!

"Wow," Tammy whispered as the bell rang. "You are absolutely the most interesting person I've ever met!"

"No doubt!" I smiled and then took off down the hall feeling like a million bucks. But before Tammy slipped into her home-room, I turned around and yelled back to her. "You are very interesting, too!"

That made her smile.

I was at my locker getting ready to go to Math when Tammy came up behind me.

"Do you think it's because she's from Kokomo?" Tammy asked without any introduction. I looked at her kind of puzzled. "Libby, I mean. Do you think that's why she thinks she can talk about you like that?"

"Kokomo Schmokomo. Home of the first canned tomato juice and the guy who came up with Clifford the Big Red Dog. We have James Dean, Tammy. James Dean! He wasn't just famous, Tammy. He was a legend! And even though nobody really knows that about us, or cares, I take that as a major sign!"

"Oh!" she said. "I just had a great idea! I think you should have a special symbol to call out 'signs' in the archives."

"That," I said as I spun us around and headed toward Math, "is a truly good idea!"

"Oh, and oh!" Tammy said.

"A double 'oh!' Wow." I smiled.

"Heidi is starting another one of those clubs," Tammy said.

"What is her problem? She used to be nice. Now all she cares about is starting clubs so somebody can be in and somebody can be out."

In unison, Tammy and I turned to each other and said, "Go PUBERTY!" And then we did a fist bump. It's a thing we do.

The bell rang and we took off at a walk-don't-run pace toward Math, which fortunately we have together.

"It's a Movie Star Boyfriend Club this time," Tammy whispered as we slipped into our chairs.

I snapped my head around and gave Tammy the "Say What?" look. And she shrugged and gave me the "Right?" look. Then the teacher started talking and we had to face forward.

Okay. So, two things:

1. Libby Chamber has been a thorn in my side for as long as I can remember. She thinks she's the only person who was ever born to be on the stage. The only reason she beat me out for Amaryllis in *The Music Man* and Annie in *Annie* is because she takes voice lessons in Indianapolis at the St. Cecilia Music Society and my parents say it's too far for them to drive me there every week. That's why I stay after school on Wednesdays and work with my choir teacher, Mr. C.

LAINEY MCBRIDE: EARLY INSPIRATIONS . . .
Mr. C. graduated from Purdue University with a degree in Music. He LIVED in New York City. He SERIOUSLY knows what he's talking about and this is what he said to me:

EARLY INSPIRATIONS ... (continued)

"Lainey McBride, singing is not just about a bunch of notes. It's about expressing the ideas and feelings behind those notes. That's what you do and that's what makes you special."

He would definitely <u>not</u> say that about Libby. All she does is sing really loud and stay on pitch.

2. Heidi Stewart has recently become the thorn in my other side. She was always ridiculously pretty and nobody ever said no to a playdate with her—not since kindergarten—but she was always basically nice. Suddenly, as of this year, it's like someone gave her a manual on "How to Be Rude, Mean, and Totally Ridiculous" and she's really doing well at following it! I mean, come on! Movie Star Boyfriend Club? How lame is that? Only a seriously beautiful girl would be able to get a bunch of normal sixth graders to go along with that one—and Heidi will! It's one of the problems with a small school. It's not like there are forty-eight other girls you can hang out with. We have twenty-three kids TOTAL in our grade. If you don't go with the gang, you don't really go with anybody! But I don't want to have a Movie Star Boyfriend, because then everyone will expect pictures in my locker and all that stuff. My locker belongs to MAEVE! She is my greatest inspiration and I am not going to take her down just so that I can hang up a picture of some fake crush. This could become problematic, because I gotta be honest, Heidi Stewart is becoming problematic. It's like "good times" in sixth grade at Fairmount Middle School all flow through her and if you aren't on the inside? You are on the OUTS!

Oh, and actually there's a third thing:

3. Tammy's idea is a good one. From now on, whenever something happens that qualifies as a sign—a signal I am destined to be famous—I will mark it like this:

While I'm at it, here are two more:

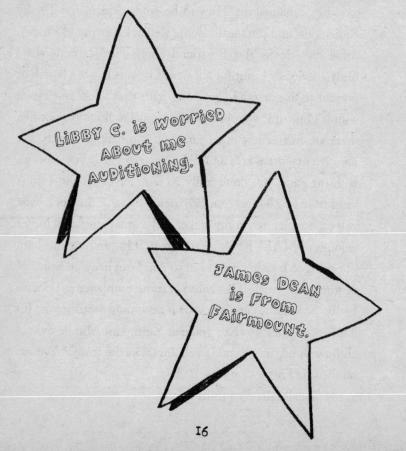

12 YEARS · # ☆ 1 MONTH 17 DAYS ☆

OMG doesn't even start to cover it!

Tammy and I rode our bikes to school today so we could go right to the library afterward to get a copy of the script for *The Diary of Anne Frank*. There really is no time to spare if I'm going to be fully prepared for my audition.

"Let's go down Adams Street!" Tammy yelled as she took off toward the back of the school. "It's faster and there's less traffic."

"Faster is good!" I yelled.

Turns out, *faster* wasn't fast enough!

"Oh, I'm afraid that book is out," Ms. Erica, the librarian, said when I leaned over the front desk, ready to tell her all about my audition.

"Really?" I said. "And you just have the one copy?"

"Well, that's the strange thing," she said as she studied her computer screen. "We do have two copies but they are *both* out."

"Can you get it from another branch?" Tammy asked. I never stop being impressed at the resourcefulness of that girl.

"Let's see," Ms. Erica said, "hmmm . . . this is weird. . . ."

"What?" I asked.

"Every copy in the county has been taken out. . . ."

Tammy and I looked at each other.

"Libby Chamber," I said in a very steady, very low voice.

"Is there something else I can help you find?" Ms. Erica said, as if this was no big deal at all.

"A way to get back at Libby Chamber," I said and Ms. Erica just smiled a little and cocked her head.

"Libby Chamber is a *snake*!" Tammy hissed as we sat on the front steps of the library and tried to figure out our next move. "Somebody needs to teach that girl a lesson!"

"Wow!" I studied Tammy's profile. "That's usually my line!"

"It's just so wrong! How could she do that? She must know that you need to have a copy of the play if you're going to be ready for your audition!"

"Exactly! And she wants me to bomb. She wants to be the only person Rodney Vaccaro notices! Well, it's not going to happen. We'll get the script some other way. We could buy it online if we had a credit card, but my parents are completely paranoid about putting their personal information in cyberspace. They are still soooo living in the nineties."

"And I don't think I can ask *my* mom right now," Tammy said softly. "It's been really hard since my dad has been gone so much. Money is a bad subject, in general."

"Don't worry about it. I have cash money of my own. We just have to get to a bookstore."

"Okay," Tammy said. "But the closest one is in Marion."

"That's only ten miles away, Tammy, and tomorrow is Saturday and the weather is perfect for a bike trip!"

Tammy looked at me sideways, like maybe I was a little crazy.

"And you know what?" I added.

"What?"

"We could pack lunches and eat under that big oak tree next to the cornfield just like we used to when we were little. That's almost halfway to Marion."

Finally, she smiled. "I love eating lunch under that oak. Why did we stop doing that?"

"We haven't." I smiled. "We're going to do it tomorrow!"

Tammy laughed and nodded. "But if we end up having to go to that theatre store in Muncie, I am not riding my bike!"

"Why? That's only *thirty* miles!" I said as seriously as possible.

"Lainey!"

"Okay!" I laughed. "I gotta get home and write that poem for Mrs. Davies's class."

We got on our bikes and rode together as far as we could. Fairmount is basically surrounded by farms on all sides. Tammy and I both live right before the southern farms start but we live on different streets, so when we got to the corner of Tyler and Main, we had to go in different directions. As I headed my way, all I could think about was the day when Libby Chamber is going to pay for all her snakiness!

One of these days, her bad behavior is going to sneak up on her and (as Nana Cake would say) bite her on the beeee-hind.

May I just say that it's a tad tense in my house these days? Dinner was a lovely combination of pork chops and knives screeching across plates. It was almost enough to make me lose my appetite. Almost. I'm not actually sure what *would* make me lose my appetite since it's never really happened. But I keep hoping.

Anyway, at least dinner is over and now Mom is doing dishes and Dad is out in the garage taking apart a motor. Chip is in his room playing the same note over and over on the trombone. Just another cozy evening at the McBride house.

That's fine, because I need to get my homework done anyway. Mrs. Davies loaded us up today because she was trying to teach us about rhyming poetry and nobody was paying attention.

Note, I said "nobody." And yet, it was my desk where her feet stopped and she looked down at me, just as I was leaning over to pass a note to Michaela because I had started telling her about my audition before class started and I needed to finish.

Mrs. Davies said, "What's so important that it can't wait, Lainey?"

"J-just telling Michaela something," I stuttered. I could feel Tammy's eyes drop to the floor. She wasn't going to be able to get me out of this one.

"Care to share with the class?"

Seriously? Didn't teachers stop saying that in, like, 1983 or something? But okay. She wanted me to share. I'd share.

"I was explaining to Michaela here that I am auditioning for *The Diary of Anne Frank* and that it's a really important production because a director who has a lot of connections in show business is going to be directing and so, if I get this part, I could really move beyond central Indiana with my career opportunities."

"And why do you want to move beyond central Indiana?" she asked.

I wasn't sure if it was a trick question or not. I mean, isn't that about the most obvious thing in the world?

"What Lainey means to say is—" Tammy bravely jumped in. I stared at her because she was breaking her own rule about interrupting a teacher in the middle of a class. She *hates* the idea of getting into trouble and so there are certain lines she just doesn't think it's wise to cross.

"No, Tammy," Mrs. Davies said. "I asked Lainey."

I could almost hear Tammy's nerves rattle.

"Because it's the only way I will become a star," I answered, and that's when Mrs. Davies went and got all quotable.

```
                   MRS. DAVIES
     Is that what you want, Lainey? To be a star?
     Or do you want to be an actress?
```

Everybody in class was silent. I heard Tammy's feet shift. I could tell she was really nervous about what I might say. She knows I find this particular question totally insulting.

The only reason I talk about being famous is because I know that being the kind of actress I know I can become will mean that I will be famous. An actress has to have an audience, right? And a great actress has to have a great audience. So, it's just simple math (which is maybe why Mrs. Davies doesn't understand, because her specialty is English).

Big Actress = Big Audience = Famous

What I finally answered was this: "I want to be a famous actress." But even that doesn't really explain it. Because being famous is different from being a celebrity and all of it's way different from being a star. But it was the best I could do in the moment.

Mrs. Davies chuckled, which also annoyed me. But I heard Tammy exhale, so I knew I hadn't blown it too bad. Regardless, even though it was Friday (!), Mrs. Davies assigned homework galore including at least six lines of rhyming poetry.

Here's mine:

Celebrity. Famous. Star.

These three words are being used
as if they're all the same,
but I'm here to tell you different 'cause
there's lots of kinds of fame.

I know you think that each of these just
wants to hear applause,
but the truth is these are different jobs
with different sets of laws.

Celebrities and Famous Folk
need only to be known.
It's just a case of timing and
how long their face gets shown.

Celebrity is fleeting, a fifteen-minute game.
Famous means it takes us longer
to forget your name.

But stars—stars are different—
they don't ask for you to know
where they are or what they are or
how big they plan to grow.

A star lights up the darkness
and inspires poetic verse,
The truth is that a real star
lights the whole big universe.

22

There are three ways to tell a star
from simple Famous Fools.
Because a star knows it's a star
and follows its own rules:

A star does not need to be known to shine.
A star is born, not made.
A star is very far away, very hard to reach,
and dangerous to touch.

So please don't try to trick me
with your questions and smirks.
I know exactly what I am
and how my brightness works!

12 YEARS 1 MONTH 18 DAYS

We rode our bikes to Marion today and things did NOT go as planned.

I mean it started out okay. Tammy and I packed really good lunches and we stopped at the oak tree as planned. We found that tree the very first time we were allowed to go on a bike ride past the famous "three-block zone" between our houses that our parents had set up when we were really little. We headed up Route 9 and right between the Scott farm and the Ward farm there's a line of trees that divides the corn and the soy fields. We claimed the front tree as ours and it's where we went every time we wanted an adventure.

"I guess this isn't exactly halfway," I said as we laid our bikes down and grabbed our lunches.

"No. I think we have about eight more miles to go!" Tammy said.

"Did you tell your parents you were doing this?" I asked.

"You mean my mom?" Tammy answered without looking up. I could actually feel her stomachache coming on. She gets stomachaches when she doesn't talk about stuff that bugs her.

"Right. Your mom. Your dad isn't home yet?" I asked, gently as I could.

"No—to both. I mean, I told my mom we were going on a bike-riding adventure but I didn't exactly say we were going ten miles away. And no, my dad's not home yet."

"I sort of told my mom the same thing." I nodded.

Then we sat there and ate sandwiches just kinda quietly because it was obvious that the subject was Tammy's parents and she didn't really want to talk about it.

I ate my sandwich and grabbed for the chips, but then I stopped myself.

"I thought you like the extra-salty kind," Tammy said when she saw me put the bag down.

"I do," I said, "but you know what Mrs. Davies says about Anne Frank. . . ."

"You're not fat, Lainey!" Tammy insisted. "You look great!"

"I know I'm not fat," I said. "But I'm . . . big."

"You're tall and really strong," she corrected. "I wish I were as tall as you. It's not so great being extra little either."

"Anyway," I said, hoping we could stop talking about size.

"Anyway, my mom and dad are both short, so I don't think I have much hope." Tammy smiled. "Let's just get up to Marion and get that script!" She got to her feet and onto her bike.

I was about to start pedaling when Tammy stopped. I turned around and looked at her.

"I don't want my parents to get a divorce," she said.

"I know you don't, Tam," I said.

Then she put her feet on the pedals and took off. That's Tammy's version of "talking it through."

We got up to speed and rode quietly for a while—well, until I couldn't stand it anymore.

"So, speaking of good times," I said.

Tammy laughed out loud. That was good.

"My parents weren't speaking last night," I continued.

25

"And this is news . . . why?" Tammy asked.

"One, it was almost midnight. Two, mom was smoking in the backyard. Three, Dad was watching TV in the family room."

"So whattya think they weren't talking about?"

"Marty," I answered without skipping a beat.

"What?" Tammy almost stopped her bike she was so shocked. "Why would they be fighting about Marty? I thought he was going to be at that school for at least another year."

"I know," I answered. "But I did hear his name come up. And Dad said it in his flat voice. Unfortunately, I didn't hear any of the words around his name. Sometimes I think you have to be a code-breaker to understand the things that go on in my house. When things go wrong nobody actually says or does very much. They just get more like they are—Dad gets Dadder and Mom gets Mommer."

"Wow!" Tammy was pointing at a sign that read MARION 2 MILES. "We really rode fast!"

I looked out at the road ahead of us. Farm field after farm field, and every now and then, a house, a barn, or a silo.

"I guess flat is good for something," I yelled in her direction.

Then we both hunched over our handlebars and pedaled hard until we were in front of the bookstore and witnessing firsthand something I never would have thought of doing in a thousand years. What we saw makes me wonder if I need to take snake lessons along with voice lessons if I'm going to be a famous actress.

Tammy actually saw her first. But when I heard her gasp I looked up and knew that thick, straight, perfect blond hair in a second.

It was Libby Chamber. She was just getting into a car that was waiting for her in front of the store and she had a good-size bag in her hand . . . from the bookstore. I felt my stomach flip and I really thought for a second I might get sick.

Just as the car pulled away from the curb, Libby looked up and saw us. She opened up her really blue eyes extra wide and smiled with the straightest, whitest teeth that have ever been grown.

"Lainey!" she shouted, and she stuck her arm out the window and waved. "Hi!"

I cannot explain why but my hand actually went up into a little wave. I guess I was in some kind of shock. Tammy grabbed my arm and pulled it down.

"You know what was in those bags, don't you?" Tammy said.

"Yeah," I said, still staring at the back end of her car as it got smaller and smaller in the distance. "I know."

We turned to each other and just stared silently for a minute.

"She always acts so nice when you actually see her," I said.

"We might as well go inside and make sure we're right," Tammy said, and she headed for the store.

"Is there any chance you have a copy of the play *The Diary of Anne Frank*?" I asked the lady behind the counter.

The cashier cocked her head and looked a little confused. "Well, I did. But a young lady just came in and she bought all of our copies."

"Just out of curiosity," I asked, "how many copies did she buy?"

"Five," she answered. "I'm sorry. I won't have more for a week or two."

Tammy and I slipped away from the counter. We walked quietly out of the store and ended up sitting on the curb where Libby's car had been.

"She has a fancy car," Tammy said.

"They're rich," I responded. "That's why she gets so many lessons."

Tammy nodded and grounded some gravel under her shoe.

"I hate to say it," she finally said, "but her eyes are an amazing shade of blue. You can actually see them from far away."

"That's true," I answered. "But they are also shark eyes. They have no life in them."

"That's true, too," Tammy answered.

FROM: LaLaLainey@yippee.com
TO: NanaFofana@ditty.com

SUBJECT: Anne Frank

Dear Nana Cake,

You will not believe what Libby Chamber did this time. I'm not even going to write about it here because I want to see your face when I tell you, but let me just say this: The girl is a snake.

And Heidi is making everyone choose a movie star boyfriend. It is so lame. I think I might just pick Al Jolson since I already have his picture, and plus, I know everything there is to know about him, thanks to you.

Are you coming to visit this month? I have a lot of rehearsing to do before my big audition and it's way easier to do with your help. (Although I don't actually have the script yet to do any rehearsing . . . thanks to Libby Chamber . . .) Tammy is a really big help but she doesn't read the other parts as well as you do. Please tell me you're coming.

Things are a little weird here but I can't tell you why exactly. Mom is busy and never seems to know what to say when I try to talk to her about my career. Dad is silent (except when he can think of something short and disapproving). Chip is annoying. And, as I believe I already mentioned, Libby Chamber is a snake. I love you and miss you.

Lainey McBride, PFP

Nana Cake says she took an early interest in show business and just never stopped. She was president of the Al Jolson Fan Club when she was nine. He was a famous singer, actor, and comedian, and they used to call him "the greatest entertainer in the world." That's why she got this autographed picture.

She gave me the picture on my eleventh birthday.

SUGGESTED ARTICLE:

EARLY INFLUENCES ON LAINEY MCBRIDE:

Lainey McBride has always had an uncanny ability to remind us of the theatrical greats who made their mark long before she was born. She may owe a thank-you to the legendary Al Jolson for that. "Al Jolson was a childhood hero," McBride once said. "His was a rare talent that survived the uneasy bridge between the silent film era and 'talkies.' I can only hope that my talent will also survive the technological advances of my own era." Among other things, Al Jolson was famous for making the first full-length talking moving picture, *The Jazz Singer*.

12 YEARS
1 MONTH
19 DAYS

I refuse to dwell on the evilness of Libby Chamber. I forge ahead!
Even though I'd love to punch her lights out!

I'm positive that my favorite store on the entire planet will
have a copy of the play, because Mr. Mankewicz at The Play's the
Thing has never not had whatever I've needed for whatever play
I'm doing.

Tammy and I will just go there.

Except that it's in Muncie, and Muncie is thirty miles away.

So—here starts Project: Get Todd to Drive Us to Muncie.

Todd is Tammy's older brother, and he's not always in the greatest mood, so the first thing we have to do is get him in a good
mood. And the best way to do that is to butter him up with his
favorite thing.

Recipe: Todd's Favorite Brownies

1 Bicycle
2 Hours to get to Hilltop* Grocery and back
3 Dollars
49 Cents
1 Shoulder bag to carry Little Debbie Cosmic Brownies home

*It should really be called Incline Grocery,
since we don't really have hills. . . .

I'm waiting for Tammy to call. She left the Little Debbies on Todd's bed this afternoon with a note that asked very politely if he would be willing to drive us to Muncie. Hopefully, Tammy's genius people skills will do the trick and he'll say yes. After all, we did spring for the 12-pack.

If she can't get him to say yes, then I'm going to have to come up with a Plan B. The clock is ticking. I need that script!

12 YEARS
1 MONTH
20 DAYS

This diagram gives you an idea of what I have to deal with in order to pursue my dream:

THIS IS CHIP'S ROOM

Home to endless trombone playing featuring such time-less classics as the trombone section of "We Three Kings" and the trombone section of "March of the Penguins" and the trombone section of just about anything, which really all sounds the same.
BLAT. BLAT. BLAT. SLIIIIDE. BLAT. BLAT. BLAT. SLIIIIDE.
And home to Chip, who truly believes that playing the trombone is more important than the demanding vocal training that is necessary for a PFP.

AUDIENCE WALL

THIS IS MY ROOM

Home to Lainey McBride and the remarkable dedication to the hard work it takes to become a legendary all-round performer. This is where Lainey McBride rehearses every afternoon by playing one song many, many times in order to sing along to that song over and over until she has perfected her lyrics, pitches, and delivery.
To be the kind of performer Lainey McBride is destined to be demands more than a couple rehearsals.

This is the ridiculously thin wall separating the monotony of endless trombone playing from the heart-racing exhilaration of a Future Famous Person preparing for her destiny.

Chip blew a gasket today. It doesn't happen very often but I always know when it's going to because I hear: BLAT. BLAT. SLIIIIDE. BANG! That "BANG!" is the slide falling

out of his trombone. It usually happens right after I've just rehearsed the big ending of an "Act One Finale" kind of ballad with
lots of pizzazz!

Anyway, I had just finished playing the part of the Irish maid
(who would soon sink) when I heard it.

BLAT. BLAT. SLIIIIIDE. BANG! I counted to three and
then—

                        CHIP
    MOM! You HAVE to tell Lainey she can't play
    the same song over and over for two hours! I
    am practicing for Band! This is my homework! I
    can't do my homework if she is going to blast
    that stupid music all afternoon!

                        LAINEY
    You are practicing for Band? Band?! I am pre-
    paring for my future!

                        MOM
    Chip, you are to stop yelling and calling your
    sister's music stupid. Lainey, you must turn
    down your music and you are not to play any
    song more than three times in a row.

    This is to be expected. Artists always struggle,
and great artists struggle greatly.

I HAVE great struggles.

33

The Early Years

Nana Cake gave me my first show album, *Fiddler on the Roof*, when I was in first grade. I went to work right away to memorize every song. I rehearsed every minute I could. One day, I came home for lunch and finished eating extra fast so I could go down to the basement to get in a little rehearsal. I was almost done memorizing "Miracle of Miracles." I just wanted to run through it a few times so I could move on to "If I Were a Rich Man" after school. Once I had all the lyrics, I went upstairs to get ready to go back to school. Except when I got upstairs, the house was quiet. My mom wasn't in the kitchen and neither was Chip. I found my mom in her room folding laundry. You should have seen her face when she saw me standing there. I didn't have a camera at the time and that's too bad, because it would have been a nice archival piece. But if I did, the picture would have pretty much looked like this.

"I thought you went back to school an hour ago!" she said.

"I've been rehearsing," I told her. Then I performed "Miracle of Miracles" for her, including the big ending.

When I was done, she stared at me for a couple seconds and then said, "That's very good. Get in the car. You're supposed to be in school."

She drove me to school and explained to Mrs. Sawyer that I had been rehearsing and she was very sorry and it wouldn't happen again. So that was the end of lunchtime rehearsals, which means after school is pretty much the only time I have to do my work.

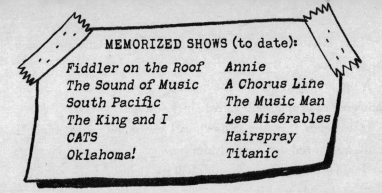

MEMORIZED SHOWS (to date):

Fiddler on the Roof

The Sound of Music

South Pacific

The King and I

CATS

Oklahoma!

Annie

A Chorus Line

The Music Man

Les Misérables

Hairspray

Titanic

It's a good start, but I have a long way to go before I will be a real expert. It won't be easy with Chip fighting me every step of the way.

And by the way, while I had Mom in my room, I decided to make my plea.

"Mom?" I asked as sweetly as I possibly could.

"Lainey?" (She answers like that a lot.)

"You know how I've been trying to get a copy of *The Diary of Anne Frank* and the very wicked Libby Chamber keeps making that impossible?"

"So it seems," she answered.

"Well, I have just one more chance to get that script in time for me to truly be prepared for the biggest, most important, truly—"

"Lainey?" Mom interrupted.

"Yes?"

"What do you want?"

"A ride to Muncie," I said, cutting to the chase.

"Ah. The Play's the Thing?" she asked.

"The best store on the planet," I said, nodding.

"I will have to look at my schedule, Lainey. That trip always ends up taking half the day and there's just a lot going on right now."

"Like what?" I asked, thinking I might finally get some information.

Mom looked at me like she didn't know what to say. Then, she shook her head and said, "Life, Lainey. Just life."

It was clear that was as much as I was going to get. Fine. "I really, really need that script, Mom."

"I understand." She nodded. "I will try, Lainey."

"Thanks, Mom," I said.

Mom went to go back downstairs but then she turned back.

"Lainey?"

"What?"

"If you'd be willing to play your music lower, you could probably get away with playing your songs as many times as you need to so you can keep memorizing all those words. But you really have to keep it low."

I smiled at Mom and nodded. She headed downstairs.

She really does like this show business stuff. I can tell.

Okay, I have to get back to *Titanic*. My voice lesson is tomorrow and I want to sing the entire maid's song without looking at the music!

FROM: NanaFofana@ditty.com

TO: LaLaLainey@yippee.com

SUBJECT: re: Anne Frank

My dear Lainey,

Libby Chamber *is* a snake, sweetie. You are correct. Therefore, you must beware because they can be dangerous. Understand? And you must decide if you are going to be a snake in return.

And yes, I am visiting. But I won't be there until the end of the month, so you will need to do a lot of rehearsing before I arrive. Do not wait for me. As I have told you many times, waiting is a dangerous frame of mind for an artist. You must stay active and in constant forward motion. If Tammy does not read the other roles well, allow that frustration to feed you as an actress. Anne Frank was very frustrated by the people around her. It could be very useful for you to feel that frustration while you are rehearsing. In fact, it sounds like you have opportunities to be frustrated all around you these days. Your mother works very hard, I know, but she does it so that you can do things like take dance classes and acting classes. You're actually a very lucky girl to have a mother who's willing to do that whether she "understands you" or not. Chip is just doing his job. Brothers are supposed to be annoying. As for your silent father, what can I say? He's been silent ever since I gave birth to him. That's just who he is.

Hang in there. We'll get everything straightened away. I love you and miss you, too.

Nana

I'm not even sure how to present what I'm about to tell you. This might be the weirdest thing ever!

I just came up to my room to check my email to see if there was any word about Todd from Tammy. I logged on to my email and—well—there was nothing from Tammy, but there was, well, I guess I'll just let you read it.

Here. This is what I just found in my inbox:

FROM: StarChamber@yippee.com
TO: LaLaLainey@yippee.com

SUBJECT: Really Sorry

Dear Lainey,

Hi. It's me. Libby Chamber.

I know you're probably surprised to see an email from me, but I hope you are actually reading this and haven't deleted it. I wouldn't blame you if you did, though. Because I know I haven't been nice to you lately.

When I saw you at the bookstore in Marion the other day, I started to feel really bad about taking all the copies of the play. I guess it seemed like a good plan at first because I know what a great actress you are and that, if you prepare, you will probably get the part. So I was just thinking about how much I really wanted to make sure I got the role of Anne Frank and not about how upset you would be. But when I actually *saw* you, I guess I finally looked at it more from your point of view.

I am SOOOO sorry, Lainey. I was wrong. So I hope you will think about forgiving me.

It would actually be kinda great to be friends. Don't you think? After all, we are the two best actresses in central Indiana. We *should* be friends. Right?

I hope you will write back.
Sorry. Sorry. Sorry.
Libby

Wacko! Right? Although not entirely. She did actually admit that I'm a better actress than her. So she's not entirely insane. But seriously? I'm supposed to just forget all her tricks and snottiness and turn around and be her BFF?

I don't think so. Time to call my *real* BFF!

This is why Tammy is my BFF. She's not only really fun and nice. She is S-M-A-R-T! This is what she said after I read her the email:

TAMMY
If she's so sorry, ask her when she's send-
ing you one of her thousands of copies of the
script!?

So sooo absolutely brilliant! I can test her honesty and (hopefully) finally get the script because (by the way) Todd still has not given us an answer. I can't do it until tomorrow though, because Mom is standing at the door *right* now saying, "Lights out!"

○ ○ ○

FROM: LaLaLainey@yippee.com

TO: StarChamber@yippee.com

SUBJECT: re: Really Sorry

Dear Libby,

Thank you for your email. I was pretty surprised when I got it, that's for sure. My friend Tammy was pretty surprised, too, and she wondered if you would send me one of those scripts since you're sorry about doing all that.

Sincerely,

Lainey

I sent this right before I went to school. It was a kinda hard email to figure out how to write. I haven't heard from her. I don't know. Maybe I made her mad. I checked my email about forty-eight times after school and then decided I had to figure out something to get my mind off of it for the moment. So I did. See?

I'm glad to announce that I've picked the shoes I will wear for the audition. Shoes are THE most important choice you can make when you're creating your character. I actually haven't ever worn these shoes. I grabbed them out of the donation pile in the basement last year when Mom cleaned out Chip's closet. It's like I was psychic. I didn't know why I took them. They just looked like good shoes for an actress to have. (Here's the funny part: They are his marching-band shoes! Ha!)

Anyway, I put them on and faced the audience side of my room. I walked around in them for a half hour and it was amazing how different I felt and how different I walked with them on.

It's tricky though, with Anne Frank, because living in that attic and hiding for her life, she wasn't allowed to wear shoes because they made too much noise. (Ugh! Every time I think about the details of her life I am more and more in awe of her. The more I learn, the more I'm amazed that she wasn't just terrified all the time. But I don't think she was. She lived her life as best as she could.)

So, I know she doesn't wear shoes in the play, but she did in her life before. I'm just using these shoes to find a way to walk that is different from how I walk, so that when I walk that way, I will feel like I'm her.

Meanwhile, ridiculousness is taking over the sixth grade at Fairmount Middle School. Okay. Maybe not the whole sixth grade, but definitely Heidi and definitely Michaela and Susan—something is happening to them. I mean, I remember things changing last year. Michaela and Sam Cody were the first boy-girl thing. They went out—whatever that means, since they actually only ever stayed in . . . the hall . . . at their lockers—for about a month. And girls started getting a little squirrely about who was invited to whose house last year, too. But this is different.

Heidi literally tackled me on the way out of Social Studies this afternoon.

"You're coming, right?" she said in a whisper, even though nobody else was around.

"Uh, coming where, Heidi?" I asked.

"To the first Movie Star Boyfriend Club meeting tomorrow," she insisted. I could not stop watching her hair bob. Heidi has dark silky hair that bobs up and down right on her shoulders. Sort of like it has a life of its own.

ANYWAY!

I said, "Heidi, it's kinda not my thing . . . it's kinda dumb." I tried to say it nice so Tammy wouldn't get mad at me for talking without my spokesperson nearby.

"Excuse me?" she said. I'll admit it. I was a little surprised at how serious she sounded.

"I just mean, it seems a little bit like, I don't know . . . like maybe we could do something a little bit more . . . I don't know . . . mature?"

Heidi stared at me with this weird expression that made it look like she was confused by everything in the whole wide world.

"Don't you get it?" she asked. "It's like actually the opposite of immature. Haven't you ever heard any of the high-school girls talking on the bus? All they ever talk about is boys—and not just the real ones. They talk about TV Boyfriends and all that stuff!"

"Okay," I said. "I guess I never heard that stuff." I think Tammy would have been proud of that one.

"I guess not!" Heidi snapped, and now it was like she was mad at me.

"Well, sorry," I said. "But I never heard anyone talk about a TV Boyfriend or a Movie Star Boyfriend and it just seems a little fourth grade if you want to know the truth."

Tammy suddenly appeared. She has the most amazing ability

to know when I'm putting my foot in my mouth. But Heidi didn't even let Tammy talk.

"I know. I know. *What Lainey means to say is*," Heidi said in a not-very-nice tone, "'I'm so busy obsessing about Maeve Winkley and stardom that I don't actually know what's going on in the real world.'"

"Wow," Tammy said. "That's not exactly how I would have put it."

"If you want to be in the club, Lainey," Heidi said, staring right at me, "you should come to the meeting tomorrow."

Then she walked away and didn't look back.

"You opened your mouth, didn't you?" Tammy asked.

"Little bit," I said. "But I really thought I was doing pretty good."

Tammy just stared at me and shook her head. Then she asked, "Are you going to go tomorrow?"

"I soooo don't want to," I answered.

"I know. But you're going to be left out if you don't. You know how Heidi can get," Tammy warned.

"Yeah. I know. But when did she turn that way? Didn't we all used to just kind of be best friends? I mean, I swear we used to like each other. Remember when we all used to hang out all summer at the pool? She was always the one who made sure everyone was invited. Remember?"

Tammy and I looked right at each other.

"Go Puberty!" we said, and then did the fist bump.

Wait. My email just beeped.

Wow. Check it out.

FROM: StarChamber@yippee.com

TO: LaLaLainey@yippee.com

SUBJECT: re: re: Really Sorry

Dear Lainey,

I'm truly glad you wrote back. I will absolutely send you a script. Just send me your address and I'll do it right away. That would make me feel soooo much better.

Libby

I'll do it. I'll send her my address. But seriously, do you think she'll send me a script? Bizarre-o!

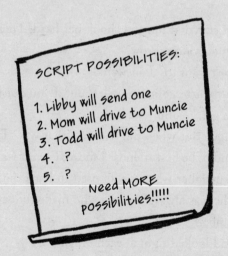

SCRIPT POSSIBILITIES:

1. Libby will send one
2. Mom will drive to Muncie
3. Todd will drive to Muncie
4. ?
5. ?

Need MORE possibilities!!!!!

Some days, all that gets me through is that when I look up at the sky, I know that I'm seeing the same stars and the same moon that Maeve Winkley sees when she looks up at the sky. For just a second, it pulls me out of Fairmount and I have something in common with someone who is truly special and at the center of everything—even if it's just for a second. Sometimes it feels like it's the only freedom I can find. I'm sorry if this isn't entertaining tonight, but it's not always a barrel of fun being born in the wrong place and growing up with people who just aren't from your planet. I'm not saying they're bad. They're just not from my planet. On my planet, you really feel everything that's going on every second of the day and you always feel like you are at the center of everything! On this other planet, you always feel like the big stuff in life is happening somewhere else, somewhere you can't get to.

RUDENESS ALERT:
I'M ABOUT TO BE MEAN. IF YOU ARE AN EXTRA
SENSITIVE PERSON YOU SHOULD STOP READING
UNTIL YOU SEE THIS:

Sometimes I hate everybody. I hate the way they don't express themselves. I hate watching them make themselves as small and unimportant as possible.

I went to the Movie Star Boyfriend (MSBF) Meeting. I picked Al Jolson. It didn't go over very well, and the little bit of niceness that Heidi had scrounged up to throw my way disappeared. Maybe it wasn't the smartest thing to do—picking Al—but I just couldn't get myself to pick Bradford Whitley or Craig Fortuna, or Avery Smith Callahan (Heidi's, Michaela's, and Susan's choices). And Tammy had already chosen Redmond Roberts—the only one I could possibly have picked and kept my self-respect.

I'm glad I picked Al Jolson. If that means Heidi makes me an outcast, then I guess that's just the way it needs to be. I've read A LOT of biographies of people who ended up being really brilliant and totally famous (and with biographies written about them—HELLO!) and a lot of them were outcasts . . . for example, Maeve Winkley!

12 YEARS 1 MONTH 24 DAYS

Okay. It's a good news–bad news situation. I'd ask you which you want to hear first, but since I won't be able to hear you, I'll just start with the bad. Get it over with.

Here's the scene: Cafeteria. Lunchtime. Today.

I was expecting a good time, because it started out so lucky when the lunch lady accidentally didn't see that she'd given me two rolls instead of one. Love those rolls. Anyway, I got my lunch and headed toward the tables looking for the regular setup, which is Tammy, Heidi, Michaela, and Susan. When I saw them, I sort of smiled as per usual and only Tammy smiled back, but she looked way nervous. She was tipping her head and brushing her hair out of her eyes over and over. Always a sure sign something's wrong. Tammy has feathered bangs and she never gets them cut often enough, so it's always an issue with the eye thing.

Anyway, I got to the table and nobody but Tammy looked up, and the other thing was this—there wasn't an empty chair.

"Hey," I said, already a little nervous. "Where's my chair?"

"I'll go get one," Tammy said, jumping up and disappearing into the cafeteria abyss.

"Actually," Heidi said, "we're sort of having a meeting of the MSBF Club and we all kind of figured you weren't really serious with the Al Jolson thing and that you didn't really want to be in it so we just wanted you to know that we're fine with that but when we have meetings it's just for the members."

"I didn't say—" I had to stop myself because actually I did pretty much say that I didn't want to be in the club, and plus, I called it immature.

Tammy came hurrying back with a chair and that same wobbly smile.

"It's fine, Tammy," Heidi said. "Lainey and I were just agreeing that she doesn't really want to be in the club, so she doesn't really belong at the meetings."

Tammy glanced from Heidi to me and she looked completely tortured. I knew what she was thinking. She was going to walk away from the table so I wouldn't have to sit alone.

"It's okay," I said. "I need to study for the science test. I was going to ask you guys to not talk to me during lunch today anyway, so this all works out really great."

"Lainey?" Tammy said, but it didn't come out very smoothly.

"Really. It's fine. Have a good meeting."

When I walked away, I could feel my cheeks start to turn beet red, the burn starting at my chin and working up to my forehead. I found a table that wasn't in view of Heidi and the rest and set my tray down. I suddenly wasn't very hungry. So I just took the two rolls and escaped out the side door of the cafeteria. I didn't really know where to go because you aren't supposed to be in the halls during lunch so I finally went to the girls' room and I found out something I never knew. There's actually a whole world of girls in the girls' bathroom during lunch. Turns out it's where all the finest outcasts eat their lunches.

Guess I know where I'll be eating tomorrow.

That, by the way, is the good news.

Tammy's really sorry about today. She said so on the phone just now.

"This is all getting really messed up," she said. "I wish you would change your mind about joining the club. It's not that big a deal and it would make everything so much easier."

A bunch of stuff flashed in my brain. I wanted to say all of it but I kept myself from talking because I could tell nothing was going to come out nicely. It felt like acid inside me. It was *really* hard to keep quiet.

Seriously? The solution is for *me* to join the club? Not for everyone else to quit? This is one of those moments when Tammy's not-wanting-to-cause-trouble is *not*-so-great.

Sometimes, trouble needs to be caused.

TGIF.

12 YEARS
1 MONTH
25 DAYS

It's midnight. I just went downstairs to sneak a couple of cookies to get me through till morning. This is what I heard:

```
                    MOM
   I'm glad he's coming home—whatever the reason.

           DAD (Sounding like a snarling dog)
              . . . whatever the reason?

                    MOM
   It's the good with the bad, Ed. I wish you
   could be happy about it.

                    DAD
   I'll be happy when he proves he knows how to be
   part of a family.
```

○ ○ ○

FROM: LaLaLainey@yippee.com
TO: NanaFofana@ditty.com

SUBJECT: Your Travel Plans

Nana! It's really late but I can't sleep and one of the reasons is I miss you. You simply must adjust your plans and get here sooner than the end of the month. Things are getting desperate.

I have several possibilities in the works to get the script but none of them are definite. If you would just get here we could go out and get the thing and start rehearsing NOW!

I suppose it wouldn't matter so much if a life in the theatre weren't my only hope to be saved from this life. But it is. It's the only way I'll ever escape from this dust speck of a town where nobody is from my planet! My artistic sensibility is suffering, Nana!

In other news:

- I picked Al to be my MSBF.
- I am officially an outcast.
- Marty is coming home. (Do you already know that?)

Write back.

Love,

Lainey

FROM: LaLaLainey@yippee.com

TO: StarChamber@yippee.com

SUBJECT: re: re: Really Sorry

Dear Libby,

How are you? Sorry to bug you but I haven't gotten that script yet. Just wondering if you know when exactly it was sent.

Lainey

I already wish I hadn't sent that. I hate sounding desperate. Especially to Libby.

12 YEARS 1 MONTH 26 DAYS

I suppose it's time I gave you a little information about Marty—even if we're not allowed to talk about him around here.

I'm not supposed to talk about the time that Marty swore at his teacher when he was in fourth grade. Or when he got a job delivering advertisement newspapers in sixth grade but actually spent a year dumping all the papers into the sewer. He only got caught because one day he lost his grip on the sewer grate and it made a giant crashing noise when it landed in the sewer. The neighbors heard the commotion and called the water department. And then, I'm also not supposed to talk about the time in seventh grade when he got kicked out of school for good because of something that is supposedly so bad that nobody will even tell me. So, I guess that's the easiest one not to talk about, seeing as I don't really know what it is.

But what I do know is that whatever he did—that's the reason why he spent the last three years at a special academy far away from home. And now he's coming home and we're back to things I don't know anything about. I mean, what did Mom mean by "the good with the bad" anyway?

Is it possible to get kicked out of an academy that you can only get into if you got kicked out of someplace else in the first place?

News Flash: This just in . . .

FROM: StarChamber@yippee.com
TO: LaLaLainey@yippee.com

SUBJECT: re: re: re: Really Sorry

Dear Lainey,

Aarrgghh! My dad is such a space cadet! When I asked him when he mailed your script, he looked at me like I was speaking French. Turns out it's still in his briefcase but he PROMISES to put in the office mail tomorrow and that always gets places extra fast! I'm so, so sorry, Lainey. I really thought it was already on its way to you!

Sincerely Sorry Again,

Libby

The Early Years

When I was in kindergarten, we lived a block from school, so we ate lunch at home. That was the year Mom read *The Wind in the Willows* during lunch every day because she couldn't stand us fighting anymore and it was the only way to keep us quiet. So lunch would be on the table when we walked through the door and Mom would start reading and she wouldn't stop until we walked back out the door. It was SOOO boring, almost worse than kindergarten. Maybe that's why I did what I did on a spring day in May—because I was so bored. Or maybe it was because I was secretly mad at Marty for causing so much trouble all the time. Anyway, this is what happened: I was walking back to school and I saw Marty ahead of me. He was playing with his friends by pulling berries off bushes and flinging them at each other. Marty never saw me that day. He never got closer than a block away and nobody ever threw a berry at me. But when I got to school, I just couldn't spend another afternoon making capital letters out of kidney beans. So I shoved myself inside my cubbie and started crying. Mrs. Hughes tried to talk to me but I was too upset to talk—only words like "berries," "boys," and "bombs" came out. Finally, Mrs. Hughes called my mom. When she got to the school, this is what I told her: "I was walking back to school when all of a sudden Marty and his friends started pulling berries off bushes and throwing them at me really hard and I couldn't get away and then the boys laughed and ran away and I ran to school." Marty got grounded for a week and I got to go home for the rest of the day. He got blamed for everything and I figured out that I was really good at acting. I never told anyone that story before. And you know what else? I never got caught. I think that's one of the main reasons I still feel so guilty about it. But what can I do now?

12 YEARS 1 MONTH 27 DAYS

I can't believe I'm actually being pushed out of my own group. I mean, Heidi and Michaela and Susan and Tammy and me? We've been together since kindergarten and we've basically always hung out together—lunch, recess, birthday parties, swimming pool, bowling, roller-skating—if one of us went, we all went. All of a sudden—I'm O-U-T! As in, Day #3 of Lunch-in-the-Girls'-Bathroom. Thank you very much.

I would probably be a whole lot more depressed about that if I didn't have a GOOD NEWS portion of the day to report. In fact this is sort of beyond good news—this is amazing news. And the curious thing is I found out about it from this tall thin girl who I saw for the first time today in the bathroom at lunch. I kind of sat down next to her to eat my rolls. She was eating something I couldn't really recognize, but she was doing it with her long, delicate fingers. It was hard not to watch her. She was quite a mysterious girl.

"I cannot wait for school to end today," she said, licking her fingers.

"What else is new?" I said, trying to be funny.

"No. Seriously. I happened to hear some interesting news about the hotel on Franklin Street."

"Like what?" I asked.

55

"Well, keep it on the DL, but I heard there are some people coming into town because they're scouting locations all over Indiana for some movie."

"What?!" I shouted.

"DL?" the girl said as she swung a long dark braid back off her shoulder. "As in, shhhh!"

"Right," I said, embarrassed. "Sorry." I hoped she couldn't tell I was hyperventilating. I tried to whisper. "What movie? What's it called? Who's in it? I'm sorry I haven't introduced myself. I'm Lainey. I'm an actress. This is very important information for me!"

"I'm Lenore," the girl said, and she sort of laughed. "You're funny." Then she added, "I know you're Lainey. You're the one obsessed with showbiz, everyone knows that. That's why I thought you'd like to know."

"You knew who I was before I introduced myself?" I asked.

"Sure," Lenore answered. "You're a highly visible person."

I never thought about the fact that people I don't know in school might actually know me because of my acting.

And—I'm a highly visible person?

I smell a "sign" coming on!

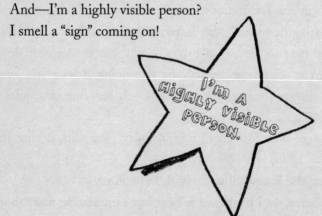

"So? Do you know who's coming? Are they big Hollywood types?"

"I don't know," Lenore said as she took a swig from her thermos. "I just know the hotel was getting rooms ready for them because they were coming in this afternoon. But you never know, might be some famous people in Fairmount!"

"How did you find out about this?" I asked her.

"Um, I know someone who works there," she said as she gathered her things and got ready to go. "She told me."

"Very cool! So I'll see you there?" I asked her just as the bell rang.

Suddenly, the bathroom filled with giggling, shouting girls and Lenore was out the door. "See ya." She waved back to me and then she was gone.

It was another hour before I could find Tammy in the hallway to tell her!

"I'm really sorry—" she started to say, and I realized I had actually forgotten about the whole lunch-table thing.

"It doesn't matter. You won't believe what I found out! There are big Hollywood people coming to Fairmount. They're shooting a movie. Scouting and staying at the Franklin Hotel. We have to go. I don't know who, but it could be huge!" I knew my words were coming out as gibberish, but I was hoping Tammy could follow. When I stopped talking and looked at her, I could tell that I'd lost her.

"What?" I demanded.

"Nothing. That's great. We should totally go!"

Weirdness. Total weirdness. "Why aren't you freaking out?"

"It's just that Heidi thought we should all go to the store for magazines after school," Tammy said to the floor.

Unbelievable. I stared at Tammy, waiting for her to tell me that she was totally going with me and not Heidi. It was quiet for a surprisingly long few seconds.

"I'll tell Heidi I can't go. This is too huge to pass up," she said. *Finally*.

"Only if you want to," I said. I tried to ignore the knot in my stomach—the one I get when my feelings get hurt.

"Totally!" Tammy said, and she smiled at me and I knew she meant it, but I also could tell she was nervous about saying no to Heidi.

The Franklin Hotel is what my mom would call "swanky." Nobody we know has ever stayed there. That's for sure. It's not surprising that this is where Hollywood would stay.

Tammy and I tried to look like we were interested in getting a room when we walked in. I tried not to touch all the furniture as I walked by, even though it all looked like it would be nice to touch.

"Front desk," I whispered to Tammy. She was staring at the chandelier like she'd totally forgotten our plan.

"May I help you?" the very tall and shiny woman behind the counter asked me.

"Um, yes," I answered. "I was hoping to find out a bit more about the movie that's being shot here in Fairmount and I heard from a source that there were some people staying here who are involved."

The lady cocked her head and smiled at me like I was a little kid. A tad annoying, but I let it slide. "You wanna be in the movies, huh?" she asked.

"I happen to be—"

"What Lainey is trying to say," Tammy jumped in, "is we're doing an article for the school paper and we just were hoping to get some information."

Nice! Tammy to the rescue.

"I see!" the lady said. "Well, I don't know that there's much of a story. At least not yet. The two people who were here checked out already, but they said they were just lookin' at lots of little towns all over the state."

"Bummer," said Tammy softly.

"Are you sure you didn't get any other information?" I asked. "Names. Titles. Anything?"

"Oh," the lady said like she was suddenly surprised. "There's one of the gentlemen, there." She was pointing toward the front doors of the hotel.

I turned around and, without meaning to, I let out a scream— just a little one—not like a horror movie or anything, but enough that it made people look at me. Rodney Vaccaro was standing at the front door of the hotel.

My brain was racing. Of course it made perfect sense that Rodney Vaccaro would be the person who would show a Hollywood hotshot around Indiana. This was one of those moments—the kind that big stars talk about when they tell their stories of being discovered. If I could make a good impression on him here, it might make a difference at the audition—not to mention whatever this movie business might end up being.

This is what Maeve Winkley says:

> *You have to grab luck when you see it or it might just slip away.*

I took a deep breath and started walking right toward him. My little scream had gotten his attention, so he was already looking in my direction. I opened my mouth to say hello, but never got a chance to actually say the word.

"Mr. Vaccaro!"

I heard the voice before I saw the person who was speaking. Rodney Vaccaro turned away from me to look toward the front door where—and I can't even believe I'm typing this—Libby Chamber was standing.

"I didn't think I'd actually run into you! It's Libby Chamber. I took your audition workshop last year in Indianapolis."

"Of course," Mr. Vaccaro said, and it sounded like he really did remember her.

I have to tell you, and I don't like to admit this, but I started to feel kind of invisible. Not only did Rodney Vaccaro forget I was standing behind him, but Libby hadn't even noticed me.

"I wanted to drop my resume off just in case there are auditions coming up for whatever this film is."

She held out her hand and there it was, the perfect-looking Libby in a perfect 8 x 10.

"Okay, Libby," Mr. Vaccaro said. "I'll take it, but there's nothing confirmed yet."

"That's okay," she said, and she flashed her sparkling smile. That's when she suddenly seemed to notice me. "Lainey? Wow! I guess everybody is here!"

I tried to figure out what to say that might get Mr. Vaccaro's attention back on me. I felt Tammy's elbow in my side.

"I guess so!" I finally said, and that felt totally lame.

"You know Rodney Vaccaro, don't you?" she asked me, smiling so sweetly that I just couldn't figure out what was going on.

"I'm auditioning for *Anne Frank*!" I blurted out, my heart racing and sinking simultaneously. "I'm really excited about it!"

"Well, that's great," said Rodney Vaccaro. "I look forward to seeing you there."

And then I nodded and tried to smile as perfectly as Libby.

"I wish I'd known you were going to be here," Libby said so sincerely. "I would have brought that script!"

I knew I should be actually talking and trying to impress Rodney Vaccaro, but I couldn't stop watching Libby. I just couldn't tell if she was doing something to trick me or if she really meant she wanted to be friends. "I have to run," Libby said. "My mom is waiting for me outside. It was so nice to see you all!"

"Always a pleasure, Ms. Chamber." Rodney smiled and he watched her as she left. Perfectly, I might add. Which is more than I can say for me.

Mr. Vaccaro turned back to Tammy and me and waited. Like he expected me to say something.

"So, anyways," I said, "thanks!"

I could feel Tammy staring at me because, duh, "thanks" was a totally inappropriate thing to say in that moment.

"I'm glad to meet you, Lainey." He smiled and then he picked up the bag that had been sitting at his feet.

"Yeah," I said. "Me too!"

Tammy's arm was on mine and she was pulling me out the door.

"Thanks?" she whispered when we got to the sidewalk.

"Just walk," I said. I wanted to get away from there before he came out of the building. "I don't know—I just got flustered when Libby showed up."

"Yeah." Tammy nodded. "You kind of clammed up. That was a first!"

"Don't remind me."

"How did she know to come here anyway?" Tammy asked in complete amazement.

"How does she do all the stuff she does?" I asked, and I really meant it. How does she know how to show up at just the perfect moment? How does she know how to leave just right? How does she get her hair to bounce and her teeth to actually shine? How does she always give great auditions when she's not even such a good actress? HOW?!

"She's really, really pretty," Tammy said softly.

"That's not helpful," I replied.

"Sorry," Tammy said.

"Cheer me up. Say something. Tell me she's not going to get Anne Frank. Tell me she's not going to haunt me for the rest of my life."

"Well"—she was thinking—"she's blond, too, so it's not like she looks any more like Anne than you do."

"You know what I really want to know?" I said, and I stopped walking.

"What?" Tammy asked.

"Is she my friend or my enemy?"

"Well, you know what I think," Tammy said, and her eyebrows arched up really high.

"What?"

"She's not your friend."

I thought about it and even though I didn't say anything else to Tammy, truth is, I'm not so sure. I think there is a possibility that Libby has had an actual authentic change of heart.

"Todd ate the brownies," Tammy said in an attempt to cheer me up. "I think that might mean he's about to give us an answer!"

"Great!" I said, but secretly, I actually believe there's a script already on its way to me . . . sent by my friend Libby.

But I wasn't going to say that to Tammy.

FROM: NanaFofana@ditty.com

TO: LaLaLainey@yippee.com

SUBJECT: re: Your Travel Plans

Hi Sweetie. Yes, I do know about Marty and I am working on clearing my schedule so I can come down there sooner. Have your parents talked to you about it? I was under the impression they hadn't talked to you and Chip yet. How did you find out? We can talk about it after your folks explain it all to you. I love you.

Nana.

P.S. Some of my best friends are outcasts! You are a rare and exceptional bird!

So? What's up with that? Nana won't talk to me about Marty until my mom and dad talk to me about Marty? Is it so top secret? And she makes it sound like she's coming down because of Marty. Not because of me. *Double* what's up with that? Nana always puts my career first.

I'm not amused. But I'm trying to look on the bright side, which is . . .

12 YEARS 1 MONTH 28 DAYS

We are in our kitchen. Dad, Chip, and I are each playing solitaire. Mom is making mashed potatoes. Nobody is talking except the potato masher and all it's saying is *squish-squish*. (NOTE TO SET DIRECTOR: Our table is silver metal and red formica. The chairs are metal with red padded seats. Everything is clean and neat but pretty worn out, too.) Anyway, back to our scene.

                    LAINEY
Nana says she's coming down earlier than usual
this month.

                    DAD
No, she's not.

                    LAINEY
Yes, she is. She told me she was.

                    DAD
And I'm telling you she's not.

NOTE TO BIOGRAPHERS:
I'm writing this whole scene in script style because it is such a perfect example of how my family can *not-talk* about just about anything. We can avoid absolutely anything. I guess it's just a natural-born gift—like it's in our genes.

Anyway, back to the scene. Mom turns and looks
at Dad. Nobody says anything. Dad starts playing
solitaire again and things get REALLY quiet. I go
back to playing solitaire, too, because I'm not
a total idiot when it comes to keeping my mouth
shut. I know how to do it when it's a matter of
survival! So I lay down a new game and I'm just
about to start playing when Dad looks over at my
cards.

                        DAD
     You'll never win. Not with that many low cards up.

   I hate it when he does that. Sorry. But I hate it so much that I
can't even keep writing it like a scene—all the negativity is block-
ing my creative flow. He tells me I'm going to lose before I even
start playing! Most of the time when he does it, I just keep quiet.
But something snapped inside me today and I finally spoke. I said
something really bad. I swear I didn't know I was going to say it
until it was coming out of my mouth.

                      LAINEY
     You don't know that! Just because you would
     lose doesn't mean that I will. I'm not like
     you! I'm going to win!

It was like an explosion the way Dad's hands banged down on the
table. All the cards bounced. He pushed away from the table and
walked back and forth across the kitchen. His limp from his back
pain seemed worse than normal. Maybe because he was getting more
and more tense as he paced. Mom finally grabbed his arm. She didn't
say anything, but she broke his trance. Chip (I know, you forgot he
was even in the room, right?) cleared his throat.

CHIP

May I please be excused?

Dad looked over at him. It was like it took him a second to understand the question. Then he nodded and Chip stood up. I decided this was one time when it might be smart to follow in my brother's footsteps.

Not only does that make a really good example of my family spending quality time together, but I also think there are similarities between my family problems and the problems Anne Frank had with her family. Even though I don't actually have the script in my hands yet, I've been researching Anne Frank so that I can internalize* her story.

Anne Frank worried a lot about getting along with her parents, too. She had trouble controlling her emotions and she said things she knew were hurtful. Too bad she didn't have a Tammy to help her.

Here's the kicker: Anne Frank didn't just keep that diary because she was going through a terrible time and was scared and confused by the world around her. She kept that diary because she wanted to be ... (I hope you're sitting down because *this* is s-p-o-o-k-y) ... FAMOUS! That's right. I read it in an actual book. Anne Frank definitely wanted to be a FAMOUS writer.

Here's what I think—Anne Frank would have become a famous writer if she'd been allowed to grow up. It wasn't just because of the incredibly terrible thing that happened to her

---

*It is essential for an actor to internalize things. That means to really breathe things in so deep that you can't get them out of you just by saying so. If you internalize something, it's in there and only comes out when you're really acting big-time! It makes you *totally* believable in whatever role you're playing. I picked up this little tidbit from Maeve. Maeve says she "breathes in all of life and lets it out one scene at a time." She is a genius.

that her writing is still important today. It's also because she was really talented and meant to be a writer and I believe her writing would have made her famous even without the tragedy. I can feel that in her because I feel it in me.

It gives me such an empty feeling right in the pit of my stomach. I think we would have liked each other.

I came to this conclusion this afternoon when I was reading in the library instead of going to Gym.

> A NOTE ABOUT GYM:
> If you'd rather crawl across broken glass than spend fifty minutes running in circles, climbing ropes, and leg wrestling—you might want to consider exploring your artistic side. Personally, I think there's a possible connection there.

This is the only award I've ever won in sports:

MOST IMPROVED PLAYER

But I won it five different times. Here's the truth about "Most Improved"—what it really means is:

> NO ONE ELSE IMPROVED MORE BECAUSE
> NO ONE ELSE STARTED OUT AS BAD.

That's fine with me. I'm an artist.

12 YEARS
1 MONTH
29 DAYS

FROM: LaLaLainey@yippee.com

TO: NanaFofana@ditty.com

SUBJECT: WHAT IS GOING ON??!!

Dear Nana,

Something is fishy around here and I know you know what it is. Plus, I know you know that I know you know. SOOOO? How come you won't tell me? Dad got REAAAALLLLY mad at me yesterday when I said you were coming early this month and then he said you absolutely were not coming early and nobody has said anything official about Marty but I totally know it's true because I am not a child and I hear things! So tell me what is going on, Nana.

My questions are:

- Why is Marty coming home when he was supposed to stay at that school for the rest of this year?

- Why are Mom and Dad fighting about it?

- Why aren't you coming early when you said you were?

It suddenly feels like everything is a total mess around here. Everybody in my family is mad at everybody else in my family— most of all, me. And the people I call my friends have me totally confused, because the ones that used to be aren't anymore and the ones that weren't are. And now all of a sudden, the ones I've never known seem to know me. AND I'M SUPPOSED TO BE PREPARING FOR THE AUDITION OF A LIFETIME AND I'M HAVING REAL TROUBLE CONCENTRATING, NANA! I'm sorry. I didn't mean to yell but don't you think the decent thing to do would be to tell me what you know so at least part of all this might start to make sense?!

Sincerely,

Your exceptionally gifted and unjustly confused granddaughter,

Lainey McBride, PFP

P.S. One of the friends confusing me is a really cool girl named Lenore. She's an outcast who eats lunch in the bathroom, too. She doesn't have any clothes that aren't black. She says it's because she is in mourning for her life. Confusing. But it sounds really cool and dramatic, don't you think?

Meanwhile, in other news, Tammy sent me an email tonight. (Because we haven't seen each other for two days. Why? MSBF Club meetings. I know Tammy just wants to be friends with everyone, but I'm starting to wonder if it's really *possible* to be friends with everyone once you get to sixth grade.)

Anyway, she says that Todd is considering the Muncie trip, which I guess is a *really* good thing because nothing has come in the mail. (Friend? Enemy? Enemy? Friend?)

Tammy says Todd's in a good mood. That's fishy. Apparently, he has been on the phone a lot, but Tammy doesn't know who he's talking to. Anyway, she said he said that he just has to check on one more thing before he can "confirm transport." If that one thing goes according to his plan, then he "will be happy to drive us to Muncie."

Happy? Todd? Like I said, fishy.

But if it takes fishy to get me to Muncie, then I'll take fishy.

☕ 12 YEARS ❀
✧ 1 MONTH ⫶⫶
❀ 30 DAYS ✧

This is what I found in a box in my locker at school today.

There was no note in the box or anything but I'm pretty sure it's Tammy's way of saying sorry for not telling off Heidi for being so mean to me. Even though Tammy hasn't really done anything wrong, I think she feels bad because she's been going to meetings every day instead of hanging with me.

I know I shouldn't be surprised. I knew making a wrong move with Heidi was going to take its toll on my social life. But I'll be honest with you, I didn't actually think it would make my best friend disappear.

Al Jolson

Anyway, I've got lots of other things to do. I had my voice lesson with Mr. C. after school on Tuesday and I've been spending lunchtime in the girls' bathroom with Lenore. And actually, Lenore and I went to a café after school today. (For the record, I've never been to a café before, but I didn't tell Lenore that.)

Lenore ordered coffee at the café.

"I started with chai in fifth grade," she said as she twirled her braid. Her fingernails were black today. "That's when I lived in Boston."

I haven't gotten the full story yet, but it seems like Lenore has lived a lot of places and she says she's "grown weary of trying to crack the shells of schoolchildren" who aren't going to like her anyway. That's why she hangs out in the bathroom during lunch. Anyway, I ordered a Diet Coke because I really don't think I like coffee. I wasn't sure how Lenore would feel about that, but she didn't judge me at all for my Diet Coke and I really appreciated that.

LENORE
One girl's chai is another girl's Diet Coke.

Lenore says stuff like that all the time. She knows how to say things so that they sound important. It might be because she's constantly reading really thick books or it might be because her dad is an artist. But it also might be because she's not from Fairmount. In fact, she's not even from Indiana. She's just here temporarily because her parents are divorced and her dad's work means he has to travel a lot.

"Usually I live with my dad," she said, "but it just so happens right now his work is taking him a lot of different places, so I have to be with my mom and she's been living in Fairmount recently because of a *relationship*." Lenore did quote marks with her fingers when she said the word *relationship*. I nodded because I didn't want to seem like I didn't totally understand. I didn't want her to feel like there was no one in Fairmount who could ever understand what she's going through.

The truth is, though, I don't really know what kind of art makes you have to travel a lot and I'm not sure if a "relationship" is the same as a boyfriend. Like I said, I don't have the whole story yet. Lenore has mysterious qualities, no doubt.

I wish I had mysterious qualities but I don't think I do. Nobody ever wonders what I'm thinking or feeling. Maybe because I'm always telling them? Something to consider.

Hold on . . . phone ringing . . .

TODD SAID YES!!! He will drive us to Muncie on Saturday!

That was the good (GREAT!) part of the phone call. The not-so-good part started when Tammy said, "You sure are spending a lot of time with the new girl. What's her name? Lenore? Where did she come from? How did you meet her? When did you become such good friends?"

I have to say, it was a little shocking since pretty much the answer to all her questions has to do with the fact that she's been spending all *her* time with "The Club."

But I am proud to say that I did not say anything about that. I just said, "Lenore is really cool. You'd like her. Maybe she could come to Muncie with us."

Probably not the right thing to say. It got really quiet on the phone. All I could hear was Tam chewing her gum.

"Did you get Sculpey Al Jolson?" she finally asked me, as if I'd never suggested Lenore go to Muncie at all.

You've got to get up *pretty* early in the morning to avoid a question better than Tammy does!

"It's so cool," I said really fast. "Thanks for making it for me."

It got quiet again and now she wasn't even chewing her gum.

I kinda wanted to avoid the whole subject, too, but I just couldn't keep my mouth shut. "Are you mad because I made a new friend?"

That's when it got REALLY quiet until Tammy took a deep breath. "I'm not mad," she said, real low and real slow and so, SO not sincerely.

"Okay," I answered (also not sincerely). "Well, thanks for letting me know about Muncie. I'm so glad he said yes!"

"Yeah," Tammy said. "So am I."

It was really weird. All of a sudden, I felt like I had to be careful about what I said, like the person on the other end of the phone wasn't my best friend since before kindergarten. When I hung up, there was a pit in my stomach like I felt when Marty first went away.

We've got trouble. I think there's a good chance that tonight's dinner will be an important scene in my biopic so I'm just going to go ahead and give you the screenplay version. Just to set the scene—there was me, Mom, Dad, and Chip in the kitchen. There were pork chops.

                    DAD
Family Work Day on Saturday.

        CHIP (With the passion of a slug)
'Kay.

    LAINEY (Spirited and with intelligence)
I can't. I have other plans.

Everyone stares at Lainey.

                    LAINEY
WHAT? I'm doing research!

            DAD (With no emotion)
Do your homework on Friday night.

        LAINEY (Polite but firm)
I'm not talking about homework.

DAD (Continuing with no emotion or expression)
Then there's no problem.

                    LAINEY
Yes, there is! There's a big problem! What I'm
talking about is more than homework. I am preparing for my audition. I need the script. Time
is running out!

        DAD (As if looking at an alien being)
Family comes first.

   That's what Dad always used to say to Marty because,
according to Dad, Marty was always thinking about himself before
the family. I almost got distracted from making my point about
needing to prepare for my audition, because it seemed like the perfect moment to ask about Marty. But I didn't. I stayed focused.

                    LAINEY
How can you say that? How can you put a
Family Work Day in front of my preparation
for my life's work?!

                MOM (Nervously)
Lainey, don't argue with your father!

                    LAINEY
I wouldn't if he would just decide that my
dreams matter and as my father he should be
just the tiniest bit supportive!

   Okay. I admit it. I knew the second it came out of my mouth
that I had gone too far. It was something about when I said "as my
father"—I sensed my dad's muscles tighten.

```
                    CHIP (Sluglike)
That was a mistake.


                    DAD (Like quiet thunder)
To. Your. Room!


                         CHIP
Told ya.


                       LAINEY
SHUT UP!
```

I believe that Anne Frank would have made the same choice about Saturday if she were forced to decide between bagging black slimy leaves and pursuing an opportunity to grow as an artist. Anne Frank never gave up and neither will I.

FROM: LaLaLainey@yippee.com

TO: StarChamber@yippee.com

SUBJECT: Script Progress

Dear Libby,

Just wanted to let you know that the script has not come in the mail. Are you sure it got sent? Anyway, I'm going to be able to get one on Saturday, so it looks like I'll be all set (even though I'm probably going to get into big trouble, but that's another story!).

Lainey

I'm not exactly sure why I just told her all that.

12 YEARS
1 MONTHS
1 DAY

The problem with having your best friend/spokesperson in charge of saying "What Lainey means to say . . ." in order to get you out of jams for saying things you shouldn't say, is this:

> When you say something you shouldn't say
> TO YOUR BEST FRIEND,
> no one is there to stop you.

I should know. Because I just said something I shouldn't have said to Tammy and there was no one there to put on the brakes. This is what happened:

I rode my bike over to Tammy's house after school today. We always read the new *People* as soon as it comes out, so I figured that would still be the plan even if a few other things have been changing lately. But when I got there, Tammy didn't pull me inside the house like she usually does, with the magazine in one hand and the Pringles in the other. Instead, she came outside and stood in the driveway. So I just stayed there, sitting on my bike, looking like a dope.

Tammy started picking up stones and throwing them at Todd's BB-gun target and this is what we said:

LAINEY

Hey.

TAMMY

Hey.

LAINEY

You got the magazine?

TAMMY

My mom forgot to get it at the store today.

I SOOO promise you that this is TOTALLY *not* true. Her mom has been getting *People* since as long as I can remember. There's NO WAY she just suddenly forgot it today. So, I just started talking and it went like this:

LAINEY

I know you're mad at me, Tammy. You got mad
when we were on the phone and I mentioned the
idea of Lenore going with us to Muncie.

TAMMY

I'm totally not mad.

LAINEY

You so are! You're mad because I'm making a
really cool new friend while you're off doing
whatever it is you have to do to stay popular
with Heidi even if it means ignoring your best
friend.

Tammy didn't say anything. She stopped throwing stones for a second and looked right at me. But then she shifted her eyes so she was actually looking over my shoulder, and then she picked up some more stones and started throwing them at the target again.

But she was throwing them harder than before. In fact, when she hit the bull's-eye, it stuck inside the target. All of a sudden, I felt really hot and really mad.

LAINEY
Why didn't you tell Heidi she was wrong for
leaving me out of the club? Why didn't you
stick up for me? And stop saying you're not
mad! You can't always make everything
okay by NOT talking, you know!

TAMMY
What do you want me to say?

LAINEY
Say you don't want to go to Muncie with
Lenore! Say you just want to go with me! Say
you'll tell Heidi I'm not a freak and that
she's really mean! Say you're mad. You NEVER
say you're mad! You don't even say you're mad
at your dad for leaving your family!

That's when the real silence started. It was big and long and deep. I started to feel sick to my stomach again and my skin got itchy.

After about six hundred hours went by, Tammy dropped the stones in her hand and looked right at me.

TAMMY
Well, I gotta go. I'll see you tomorrow.

Tammy turned around and walked into her garage. I just stood there listening to the door open and close and feeling like the meanest girl in the world.

But here's the amazing thing. Tomorrow, I'll show up here to go to Muncie and, as long as I pretend like this didn't happen, Tammy will act like it didn't happen. And that's what Tammy will want me to do. No doubt.

Tammy is a better person than me. She's way nicer. But I'm definitely more honest about my feelings.

HISTORIC NOTE:

Dear Family Work Day People,
I know you do not understand why I cannot help you today and I'm sorry about that. Because if you did, you would not expect me to rake leaves instead of making the very important trip to Muncie to get a copy of *The Diary of Anne Frank* so I can continue my growth as an artist of the theatre.
Sincerely,
Lainey McBride

*12 YEARS *2 MONTHS 2 DAYS

I have it! I have my own copy of the script for *The Diary of Anne Frank*!

I must say a word here about Todd. I'm not sure Tammy and I have been entirely fair about him. Turns out, he is a very supportive person. Because of what he did for me today, I will be adding him to my list of people to thank when I accept my first Oscar (or Tony, whichever happens to comes first).

OSCAR and/or TONY
Thank-You List:
Nana Cake
Maeve Winkley
[director]
[writer]
[producers]
[agent]
Mom
Dad
Chip
Marty
Tammy
Mr. C.
Miss Margy
Madame Ava
Todd

It took us about twice as long as it should have to get to Muncie because there was road construction and all the traffic was stopped up. But Todd just turned up the stereo.

"Can't let a little traffic jam stop us!" he said. Tammy and I tried hard not to giggle, because he was being just plain cheerful and that is definitely not normal for Todd. Truly weird.

But what wasn't weird was Tammy and me. We were in the backseat and it was like nothing ever happened. It was so nice just to be with my best friend again!

Anyway, during the ride to Muncie, we didn't dare look at each other, because of the rearview mirror and Todd being able to see us. We were afraid we might crack up. So we pressed our knees against each other because we had to do something to deal with the fact that we now understood WHY Todd was in such a good mood.

See, Tammy and I weren't just in the backseat for our health. We were in the backseat because the front seat was taken—by Cindee Binney, High-School Cheerleader.

She was sitting next to Todd. I mean, RIGHT next to Todd thanks to the fact that Todd has a *really* old car where the front seat goes all the way across just like the backseat. In fact, Cindee was sitting so close to Todd that actually both Tammy and I could have fit in the rest of the seat that was left over. But that's okay. Todd was happy and Cindee was giggling and we were going to Muncie.

"So, like, you're gonna try out to be in a skit?" Cindee asked me. She was cranked around and looking at me kinda dopey. I think really the only reason she was asking me was because when she turned around to face the backseat she actually got to sit in Todd's lap for a second.

"It's not called 'trying out' and it's not called a 'sk—'"

"What Lainey means to say," Tammy cut in, "is yes. She's trying out for a skit and we're going to get the book that has all the lines in it."

Cindee Binney giggled. "That's cute!" she said, and then she spun back around and slipped off Todd's lap.

Tammy turned just a little bit toward me. I didn't turn my head, but I could see her enough from the corner of my eye. She raised her eyebrow and lowered her head and giggled really quietly. I giggled really quietly back. So GREAT to be with your best friend!

Plus! Look what Tammy gave me when we got in the car:

SCULPEY ANNE FRANK!

Didn't I tell you? The girl is a genius!

After about a gazillion more giggles and "That's cute!'s" we got to Muncie. I don't want you to get me wrong. I know Muncie is only Muncie. It's a small town and not much happens there. I know the difference between big cities and small towns. But even so, I always feel just a little bit more excited when I'm there. Compared to Fairmount, it feels pretty big and busy.

Anne Frank

Todd pulled over to the curb.

"So do you know where the store is, Lainey?" he asked. He was smiling so much it was actually getting a little creepy.

"Yup. It's called The Play's the Thing," I said. "It's on South Main, right around this corner. We could just get out here and walk. We'll go get my script and meet you guys back here later."

I really wanted Tammy and me to walk into The Play's the Thing by ourselves. No supervision necessary. Not when it comes to my career. I need to be treated with respect and I don't need a babysitter.

The Play's the Thing is the real deal. It is a serious store for serious theatrical people. It is not a place in which I want to be treated like a child—unless of course the word is being used as an adjective—as in, *child star*.

"Awesome!" Cindee squealed, and she leaned real hard into Todd.

The next thing I knew, Tammy and I were walking by ourselves down South Main in Muncie and laugh at me if you want, it felt really cool.

After we were around the corner and out of sight of Todd and Cindee, I said, "Gross."

And Tammy said, "Totally."

Then we were standing in front of The Play's the Thing.

I love this store. It's got EVERYTHING! The front counter has tons of stage makeup, which is way heavier than regular makeup, and you wouldn't believe how many amazing posters from actual Broadway shows are on the walls. In the back they have the gels and different kinds of gobos that lighting designers use to make patterns and designs with the lights. There's glow-in-the-dark spike tape and about a hundred other colors of tape that stage managers use to mark a rehearsal floor. Plus, there's one whole aisle with the just about one billion things that stage managers always have in their bags.

Stage-manager bags are amazing places. I remember looking through one once when I was in *The Music Man*. There were eight pens all rubber-banded together, a box of colored pencils, a measuring tape, six different kinds of Band-Aids, a stack of schedules, hair bands, a stopwatch, a dictionary, a bunch of drawings of the set, three different binders, a tape recorder, and Post-its in five different colors. And that's just the stuff I can remember.

There's another aisle in the store with supplies for set designers to build model-size sets before they build the real ones. There are three aisles of props and costumes and special-effects stuff that makes things like smoke and fire and rain and snow look real on-stage. And there's an aisle for books about acting and lighting and designing and directing and producing and casting and auditioning and once I even found a Maeve Winkley biography, unauthorized.

It was excellent.

The scripts are filed alphabetically by playwright in file drawers behind the front counter.

I could just about live in this store.

The door hadn't even closed behind us when a really cranky voice said, "Whattya want?"

It didn't surprise me, because I knew who it was. Arthur Mankewicz. He's the old man who runs the store. He isn't exactly friendly. I've always assumed he was bitter due to a life in the theatre gone bad. So I always treat him with extra kindness even when he's rude to me.

After all, I still have a future and he doesn't really anymore.

"I need a script," I say, putting on my sweetest voice.

"Do you care which one?" he cracked.

"*The Diary of Anne Frank*, sir," I say. "I'll be auditioning for the role of Anne."

"Uh-huh."

He went behind the counter to the huge file drawers. I have to stop here for a show of respect to Mr. Mankewicz. He never has to look up the name of a playwright. When you tell him which play you want, he always goes straight to the right drawer. I think he knows every play that was ever written and the name of every playwright who ever wrote those plays.

He opened the drawer second from the top. Then he went script by script, muttering to himself.

I think those drawers are amazing. It's like the history of everything that matters, in alphabetical order.

"I'll find it!" he snapped at me without looking up.

"That's fine, sir. I'm happy just to be in your store."

"Hmph."

Tammy was in the set-design aisle which has all the stuff the designers use to build their tiny models.

"This stuff is really cool," she whispered. "I could make a whole world just for my Sculpeys."

"Wow!" I said. "That's an excellent idea!" I suddenly felt the need to say something really nice to Tammy. "You see ways to make things that nobody else does, you know that? I think it's really cool."

Tammy looked at me funny. I don't compliment her as much as she compliments me. I really need to work on that. I think there's something about The Play's the Thing that just makes me a better person. I'm kind to mean people and extra supportive of my best friend when I'm in that store. I feel happy.

"Here," the old man croaked. "You want it?"

"Of course I want it, sir!" I exclaimed. "You've made me the happiest girl in the world!"

"A perky Anne Frank. Not sure how that's gonna play," he said.

Now, I don't usually consider *perky* an insult, but the way Mr. Mankewicz said it? It was like he just ate something really nasty or something.

Even so, I couldn't help but smile. Because Mr. Mankewicz and I are both theatre people and that feels good.

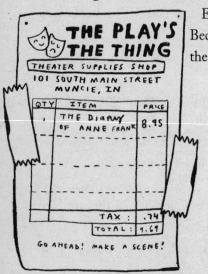

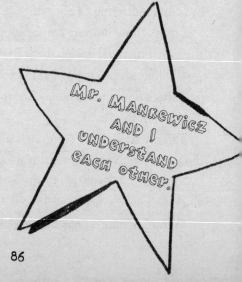

Mr. Mankewicz and I understand each other.

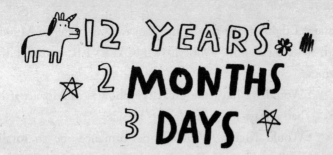

12 YEARS 2 MONTHS 3 DAYS

If you are a screenwriter and you are reading this archive because you're making my biopic, then you'll have to write the scene that took place when Todd and Cindee and Tammy dropped me off after our trip to Muncie completely and totally with description.

Set it in the front yard. Have my Mom and Dad and Chip hold rakes. Make them glare at us while we're in the driveway. The page should look like this:

```
                         DAD

                         MOM

                         DAD

                       LAINEY

                        CHIP

                       LAINEY

Lainey exits to her room.
```

Nobody has really talked to me today, either. Mostly it has just been long hard looks of deep disappointment.

But before I get to that, let me just say right now that I

understand I didn't make the "right" choice about going to Muncie instead of doing Family Work Day. HOWEVER, consider the following:

- Would we have the great symphonies of Mozart if he had always made the "right" choice?
- Would Maeve Winkley's performances be so totally brilliant if she always made the "right" choice?
- Would Anne Frank's diary be so important if Anne was a girl who always made the "right" choice?

I think not.

Art has its own demands. Sometimes those demands are not going to fit in perfectly with Family Work Days.

Oh, and just FYI, not that you'll be surprised: I'm grounded and the terms are harsh.

Duration: One week.

Exclusions: School and Mr. C.

Confines: In the house from after school until morning.

Terms: No TV. No phone.

FROM: NanaFofana@ditty.com

TO: LaLaLainey@yippee.com

SUBJECT: The Situation

My Dear Confused-Yet-Persistent Granddaughter,

I am not going to discuss this with you if your parents have not discussed it with you. (You're already in hot water. There's no need for both of us to get into trouble! Ha-ha!) I'm sorry things feel so difficult right now. I will try to find a chance to encourage your father to speak to you so that things start looking a little clearer, but that's as much as I can do. (He has never much listened to his dear old mother, you know.) As for me coming to visit, I've been asked to wait until things calm down. And as for what I care about—your career or other things—I care about you and your brothers and your mom and your dad, Lainey. Don't confuse ambition with what you really care about. That's bound to lead to the kind of trouble you'll never be able to solve. Stay calm. Your father doesn't express himself very well. I know that's hard. But he's a good person and he does love you. More soon.

Love,

Nana.

P.S. Lenore sounds quite interesting. When she told you she was "in mourning for her life," she was quoting a line from the play *The Three Sisters* written by a famous playwright named Anton Chekov. Sounds like she might be almost as theatrical as you! See how good things can happen from the strangest of circumstances—like eating lunch in the bathroom? (Is that really necessary, by the way? I do hope you're washing your hands.)

THINGS ARE CLEARLY GOING FROM BAD TO WORSE! Nana has NEVER done exactly what her son (my dad) tells her to do. Even if he doesn't listen to her, she has always told him when he was being too strict or not understanding. And what was that business about "ambition" and "caring"? Do I have to remind her that she's the one who said:

> *If you're going to go after a big dream, you have to want it more than anything!*

And what's up with all that Suzy Sunshine kind of "good things happen from bad things" talk? And by the way, Nana, YES! I really DO have to eat in the bathroom. The old Nana would have understood that!

HELLO?! Who are you and what have you done with my Nana?

Wait till I tell her about being grounded. That'll snap her out of this. She, for sure, will understand why I had to do what I did to get the script. No doubt!

Hold on a minute. Mom is knocking on my door.

Okay. It's five minutes later and I'm a little surprised and apparently even more in the doghouse than I was.

Turns out I got a package in the mail yesterday while I was "missing in action." Yup. From Libby Chamber. With a note on the outside of the package that said:

Sorry it took me so long to get this script to you. Happy rehearsing!

Why did she have to write it all on the *outside* of the envelope? Especially now, of all times! I'm telling you—that girl and her timing!

"If you could get a script in the mail like this then it makes it even more disappointing that you disobeyed us yesterday and let your family down."

Just another feel-good moment, ladies and gentlemen.

"I didn't know, Mom" was the best I could do—it would have been too hard to explain that I wasn't sure if I could trust Libby or not. "I'm sorry everyone is so disappointed in me."

"That's different from actually being sorry, Lainey."

Ugh.

Then she turned around and left. And the thing that made me feel the worst? She closed the door very calmly and quietly. I don't know why that felt so creepy, but it did. It would have felt better if she'd yelled her head off and slammed the door.

Even when Libby is nice—trouble seems to follow.

I'm glad it's Sunday. School will be a relief.

12 YEARS 2 MONTHS 4 DAYS

What everyone seemingly fails to realize is that I have an extremely important audition in less than two weeks and the specifics of this grounding are making it very hard to prepare.

I did wrong. Okay? I said I was sorry. Even if it wasn't exactly like Mom wanted it, I still said it.

But it isn't just Mom and Dad. I'm not even getting support from my strongest supporters.

```
                    TAMMY
You mean you didn't get permission to go to
Muncie!?! Are you kidding!?!?

                    LAINEY
Wow, Tam. You almost sound like you're mad!

                    TAMMY
It's not funny, Lainey.

                    LAINEY
You don't have to tell me that! I'm in isolation
at the exact moment we need to be preparing for
my audition!

                    TAMMY
That's not what I mean.
```

LAINEY

Then what do you mean?

TAMMY

You could have gotten Todd in a lot of trouble.

LAINEY

What are you talking about? Todd was thrilled
to go to Muncie . . . with C-I-N-D-E-E . . .
Remember?

TAMMY

Lainey, what if your parents called my parents
and Todd got blamed for driving when all he was
doing was a really nice thing for you?

LAINEY

Wow. Thanks for the support.

So much for the return of our best-friend status. I could NOT
believe how mad she got at me—and all because she was defending
TODD? I guess she really is deep-down mad at me about Lenore.
That's what happens when you don't express your emotions. They
end up coming out all sideways, about stuff that doesn't even make
sense.

But Tammy wasn't the only shocker of the day:

LAINEY

. . . and that's what happened, Mr. C.! I made
the choice of a serious artist and now I'm being
punished for it.

MR. C.

Actually, Lainey, I think you're being punished
for disobeying your parents, shirking family
responsibility, and crossing the county line
without your parents' permission.

                         LAINEY
     Well that's a very nuts-and-bolts way to look
     at the situation. Don't you think?

I know exactly what you're thinking and I was shocked, TOO!
Mr. C. has always been the coolest teacher in school. No doubt!
This is the trouble with middle school. No matter how cool and
unique you are when you go in, if you don't have an escape route,
you'll come out in a box looking like everybody else. The new and
interesting fact here is that it works on teachers, too. Even they get
turned into big blocky squares who can't tell art from bad behavior.

In a Rare Moment of Telephone Relief granted by my mother
after tearful begging:

                         LAINEY
     It's persecution, Nana.

                       NANA CAKE
     Is that so?

                         LAINEY
     Totally. I'm being persecuted because of my
     artistic pursuits.

                       NANA CAKE
     What does *persecute* mean, Lainey?

                         LAINEY
     You don't know?

                       NANA CAKE
     Yes, I do know. I'm wondering if you know.

                         LAINEY
     It means I'm being tortured because I'm
     special.

                            93

Silence.

                    LAINEY
Hello?

                  NANA CAKE
Yes. I'm here.

                    LAINEY
What's going on, Nana? You're always on my
side.

                  NANA CAKE
I'm on your side when you explore what's
special about you. I'm not on your side when
you stop respecting what's special about
everyone else.

This is a turning point, people. *You* know how wrong this is.
I know how wrong this is. But apparently, no one else does—
except Lenore. I have never been so shocked and disappointed in
my whole life—by everyone. This is seriously not funny. My audition is in two weeks and nobody is helping me prepare. An actor is
not an island. An actor is a collaborative artist. This is a team sport,
and my entire first string is sitting on the bench.

I'll tell you one thing—if I were famous, nobody would dare
ground me.

But as I said, Lenore is someone I can depend on. When I told
her about what Tammy said, she really came to my defense.

"Lainey! You *have* to stop caring what those girls think of you.
They are all the same and they'll *never* understand you! I can't
stand that Heidi girl. She's ridiculous and any girl who follows her
around like a puppy is ridiculous, too!"

I didn't say anything because it didn't feel so good to talk about Tammy behind her back, even if we were sort of fighting. And, Lenore was being pretty harsh. But what happened next made it pretty hard not to agree with Lenore.

The bell rang. We opened the door of the girls' room and there was Heidi, Michaela, Susan, and Tammy. We all just kind of stared at each other like we weren't sure if we knew each other.

Michaela giggled. "Oooh, look! It's the bathroom buddies!"

There was this strange quiet second before Heidi let go with a loud laugh. Not surprisingly, Susan joined her. I looked at Tammy and waited to see what she would do and the fact is, she didn't do anything. She just looked at the floor as Heidi, Michaela, and Susan walked right between Lenore and me to get to the bathroom.

Then Lenore stared right at Tammy and said, "Better get in there. Heidi Almighty is waiting!"

I didn't know I was going to do it, but I actually laughed.

I mean, Heidi Almighty? That's pretty good, right?!

But then I saw Tammy's face and I swear, she looked like she was about to cry right there in the hallway. Lenore was glaring at her and my stomach felt like it was about to flip.

Not the best day, folks. Really. Not the best day.

FROM: LaLaLainey@yippee.com
TO: StarChamber@yippee.com

SUBJECT: THANK YOU

Hi Libby,
The script came in the mail this weekend, so I wanted to say thank you. As it turns out, I did get to Muncie like I said I was going to, so now I have two scripts! But that's great because it

means that I can use one and the person who helps me rehearse can use one. Even though I'm not sure who that person is since I seem to have lost my best friend and, plus, I'm grounded. Anyway, I don't know why I'm telling you all this. Maybe I'm starting to go crazy just like people in jail do when *they* are in isolation! Ha! Anyway, it was really nice of you to send me the script.

Lainey

12 YEARS 2 MONTHS 5 DAYS

Dear Friends, Fans, and Biographers,

I hope you're sitting down because what happened today in the hallways of Fairmount Middle School is truly beyond belief. I will tell you everything, but let me sum it up with this:

Me and Lenore: 1
Heidi and ALL her Club Girls: 0

Lenore and I were walking to gym totally minding our own business. I can say this for certain because we were talking about art, and there's nobody else in the whole school who would be interested, so we MUST have been minding our own business. All of a sudden, I hear Heidi's voice behind us.

                    HEIDI
    Look. It's the Bathroom Buddies!

Lainey keeps walking and tries to ignore Heidi,
who keeps talking.

                    HEIDI
    Isn't it amazing how freaks always seem to find
    each other?

Lainey stops, unable to believe what she's hearing.

                              LAINEY
What kind of a lame comment is that, Heidi?
I think you've been watching too many movies
on the Disney Channel. Nobody actually makes
comments that stupid in real life.

                             MICHAELA
Yes they do!

I was about to double over in laughter. Michaela thought she
was backing up Heidi Almighty, but really? She just agreed that the
comment was stupid! It stopped being funny, though, when I saw
Tammy trying to sneak behind Susan Sanchez so she could disappear behind the row of lockers nearby. She froze when she saw me
see her.

                              HEIDI
Why do you always wear black?

I nudged Lenore. I wanted her to say she was in mourning for
her life. I wanted her to call her Heidi Almighty. But she didn't say
anything.

                              HEIDI
Is it so the dirt doesn't show from sitting
on the bathroom floor during lunch? You know,
when you guys sit around and say mean things
about me and my friends just because we aren't
freaks?

I started to panic. Who had heard us in the girls' room? What
did they hear? Tammy wouldn't look at me. Tears were really close
to coming out of my eyes. I had to totally focus on biting my lip to
keep them from falling.

                    HEIDI
I thought you guys were so artistic and expressive.
You sure don't seem very expressive to me.

   I pulled my eyes off Tammy. If she wanted to be part of Heidi's
world, then so be it. It was obvious she and I weren't friends anymore.

Heidi Almighty glares at Lenore.

                    HEIDI
Where did you come from, anyway?

                    LAINEY
She just moved here. Is that against
your precious rules?

                    HEIDI
No. Just being freaky is.

Heidi laughs and so does Michaela.

      TAMMY (In a ridiculously low whisper)
Heidi.

      LAINEY (In the opposite of a whisper)
Careful, Tammy. You might actually express an
opinion. It might seem like you're upset with
someone!

Lainey looks each girl right in the eye.

                    LAINEY
You're all so busy being in your club and
making sure there are plenty of people who feel
left out, I'm not surprised you don't have time

to realize that Lenore is an amazing person.
She won't spend the rest of her life being a
nobody from nowhere doing nothing! Not like
you!

I don't know exactly when it was that the principal showed up.
I have a feeling she didn't catch any of the extraordinarily creepy
things that Heidi said. I think, based on what happened next, she
must have just shown up in time to catch my final monologue.

That was unfortunate.

"Lainey McBride," I heard from behind me. "My office, please."

And then, this is what happened:

                    MRS. PATCHUCK
What was that, Lainey?

                    LAINEY
What was what, Mrs. Patchuck?

                    MRS. PATCHUCK
That little speech you just gave out in the
hall.

                    LAINEY
You didn't hear what Heidi said, Mrs. Patchuck.
Do you realize who she really is? Do you real-
ize how she treats people?

                    MRS. PATCHUCK
We're not talking about Heidi. We're
talking about you. I don't appreciate the negative ways in which you were speaking. It shows
a lack of respect for your classmates.

                    LAINEY (Speechless)

I'm speechless here because what can I possibly say? ME? ME?!? I show a lack of respect? What about Heidi?!

                    MRS. PATCHUCK
     Now, I know you're a smart girl, Lainey.
     I trust we won't have to have this discussion
     again?

Lainey nods.

                    MRS. PATCHUCK
     Excellent. Get to class.

Have I mentioned I despise the Public School System?

P.S. I didn't notice we had a "discussion." Seems to me, Mrs. Patchuck talked, I tried to respond, she shut me down, and then she talked again.

Sooo thankful for Lenore right now. Who would have ever guessed my soul mate was waiting for me in the girls' room?

I think we're both feeling closer to each other since yesterday's battle. In fact, she invited me over to her house today for the first time. I've been dying to go to her house, but of course, I can't go because I'm still GROUNDED!

MY soul mate is an artist, too.

"My father would never do something like that," she said. "I'm so sorry, Lainey. You do not deserve to be stuck in the midst of such mediocrity. If only you were born from an artist—as I was."

I *really* wanted to ask her what exactly that meant. What kind of artist was she born from? But there's something about Lenore that keeps me from asking many questions. Besides, I think I should have been able to figure it out by now, because she's talked about him a lot. But the trouble is—I don't understand most of what she says and I don't want her to know, so I just nod and say, "That is so true." For example:

LENORE
My father's work suffers for the very reasons
it should succeed. While other artists create

work that only mimics what has already been
created, my father is a complete original. He
says the collective consciousness has been
buried beneath Dadaistic garbage created by
artists who are nothing more than copycats.
He says the true artist explores the outer
spectra of reality. A true artist lives inside
cosmic confusion because that is where real
inspiration lives.

                    LAINEY
That is so true.

I looked up *Dadaistic* when I got home. It means "in the style
of a nihilistic art movement founded in Western Europe and the
US in the early twentieth century." In other words, I still don't have
a clue what Lenore meant. But is cosmic confusion the same as
regular confusion? Because if it is, then I TOTALLY understand
that part.

So, I'm not sure if her dad is an artist like a painter or an artist
like a writer or maybe he's a sculptor . . . ? I really don't have any
idea. But I am clear on the fact that he and Lenore are both really
positive he is a genius and I believe them. I wish I could go over to
her house. I feel like there would definitely be clues there.

This is not the first time I've gotten in trouble this way. It's happened a few times with Madame Ava during acting lessons. Once
she was talking about a Russian acting teacher named Stannislofski
(I really don't have any idea how that's spelled) and "the dangers
of memory versus imagination" when it comes to "method acting."
I got a little lost with that conversation, too, but instead of telling
her that I didn't really understand what she was talking about, I just
nodded and said *hmmmm* whenever she slowed down.

The trouble with this approach is that since people think you
understood the first thing, they keep going to the second thing,
and pretty soon you have to pretend you need to use the bathroom
or that your mom wants you home or *anything* just to get out of
it. And then you have to be really nervous the next time you see
that person because what if they want to start up that conversation
again?

(I finally looked up *method acting* when I got home. It is a
technique where actors do deep relaxation to help them bring up
emotions based on their memories, not by thinking of them—but
by re-creating them through the five senses. Cool, huh?)

I'm starting to wonder if there might be a better way to
handle these moments.

Anyway, back to Lenore. Here's what else happened during
lunch today. It was very cool. We were sitting under the sinks eating our lunches when she suddenly turned toward me and put her
hands on my shoulders. She looked me right in the eyes and said,
"I see the depth of your perception, Lainey. You are I are the same.
Artists—mutants, if you will—in a pedestrian world."

It was a very intense moment. Perhaps the most intense I have
ever had in the girls' bathroom.

Then she said, "As soon as this terrible injustice comes to an end and you are no longer grounded, I will be at your side, Lainey McBride, and we will prepare you for that audition."

"I'm going to give you my second script, Lenore, because you are the one who I can depend on."

It was deep.

12 YEARS 2 MONTHS 7 DAYS

Turns out Mrs. Patchuck called my parents yesterday. Nice.

That reminds me. I'm starting a list of people I will NEVER thank, no matter how many awards I get. I look forward to the day when one of the people on my NO THANKS list fights to get to the front of the crowd as I walk by on the red carpet. They will shout out my name and I will turn very slowly and look them right in the eye. I will smile extremely glamorously and say, "I'm sorry. Have we met?"

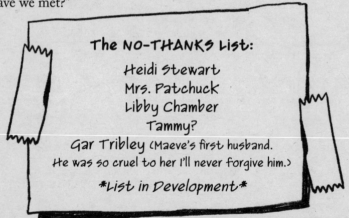

The NO-THANKS List:
Heidi Stewart
Mrs. Patchuck
Libby Chamber
Tammy?
Gar Tribley (Maeve's first husband.
He was so cruel to her I'll never forgive him.)
List in Development

So anyway, Mrs. Patchuck is on that list now because she didn't exactly do me any favors by calling my parents on the last day of my grounding to inform them that I had been "disrespectful of my fellow students while standing in the hallway today."

My dad was just about as willing to hear what I had to say as Mrs. Patchuck had been.

DAD
There are REAL problems in the world, Lainey.
When are you going to wake up and realize
nobody needs all your extra drama?

LAINEY
But, Dad—you didn't hear the whole—

DAD
I don't want to hear your self-centered
excuses, Lainey. You've been walking around
this house with an attitude for weeks as if
you're better than everyone else. Now you're
doing it at school. I'm telling you here and
now, it's going to stop, young lady! And if
you're smart, you'll make up with Tammy.
She's been a better friend to you than you've
deserved a lot of the time!

After that, Dad left. I was so mad I couldn't even speak, even though my head filled up with a thousand things I would have liked to have said if only he had stayed long enough for me to say them.

THINGS I DIDN'T SAY:

Thanks for your support, Dad, it feels great!
(NOT REALLY.)

You know what I've heard, Dad? Some fathers
actually decide to stand by their kids when
times are tough. Isn't that ridiculous?
(NOT REALLY.)

```
AND:
I hate you!
(Possibly REALLY!!)
```

I started feeling that thing I felt in the hallway at school when I saw Tammy standing with Heidi's club and I knew I was going to cry. That's what I was doing when I heard the door to my room open.

"Leave me alone!" I shouted into my pillow.

"It's Mom, Lainey."

That's when more unexpected stuff came out of me.

"Heidi Stewart started a club and kicked me out of it and told everyone to treat me like I'm a freak or something and everyone is doing it . . . including Tammy! There's no surviving sixth grade once Heidi Stewart turns on you! And why do there have to be clubs, anyway? All they do is leave people out!"

Then my mom sat on my bed and I grabbed her around the neck and held on really tight while these big, giant sob noises came out of me.

I hate this. I hate feeling alone. I hate feeling wrong. I hate feeling weak.

Today is the first day of the rest of my life. Yesterday was then. Today is now. We're moving on.

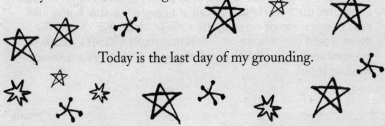

Today is the last day of my grounding.

For some reason, it appears I'm not getting any further punishment for the whole Mrs. Patchuck business, which I don't quite understand but am not planning to question. Dad didn't say a word when I saw him this morning. Just got his coffee and went out to the garage. I guess whatever he wanted to say he said last night and he's done with it. And the only thing Mom said was, "Finish your eggs. We're done wasting food around here."

That's when Chip picked up his bowl and licked it like a dog till it looked like it had already been through the dishwasher. On top of being annoying, he's weird.

Whatever.

All I care about is that I'm almost free and now I can talk to Lenore about going over to her house to rehearse!

FROM: StarChamber@yippee.com

TO: LaLaLainey@yippee.com

SUBJECT: I'm back!

Hi Lainey!

I'm so glad the script finally got to you. I was sooo mad at my dad that he kept forgetting. But now you have two, which will be really helpful, I'm sure. Sorry it's been so long since I've emailed. I was in trouble, too, and wasn't allowed to be on the computer for a week! Just because I needed to stay home and rehearse instead of wasting my time in Math! (Who knew my mom would come home at lunch that day?) ☹ Guess we have even more in common than we thought! ☺ Hope you're out of trouble soon!

Libby

12 YEARS.
2 MONTHS
9 DAYS

This is what I have found out in the last twelve hours thanks to Mom finally having a "sit-down" with Chip and me:

1. Dad is leaving on Monday to pick up Marty at school.

2. He's bringing Marty back at the end of the week.

3. Dad has been permanently retired by the army—that's *by* the army—as in, not Dad's choice.

4. The reason Marty is coming home is because we can't afford his school anymore—turns out the army was paying for it (or something like that).

5. And we also can't afford some other things, too, but I'm not totally clear on what those things are. But that probably explains why everybody has to finish their eggs now, no questions asked.

6. Mom says not to talk to Dad about the army because he's still getting used to everything that's happened. I think that's code for "Dad is seriously depressed and he'll bite your head off if you mention the reason why."

7. Mom also said we have nothing to worry about and everything is going to be fine, which is also code. That means "Mom is seriously scared, and she's not sure how this is all going to work out."

8. Nana is F-I-N-A-L-L-Y coming when Dad and Marty get back. (Hopefully, when I see her face-to-face, the old Nana will reappear and not that person who's been emailing me all the Suzy Sunshine business.)

FROM: LaLaLainey@yippee.com
TO: StarChamber@yippee.com

SUBJECT: re: I'm back!

Hi Libby,

Really sorry to hear you got in so much trouble just because you were focusing on your artistic work. My friend Lenore and I talk about this kind of thing all the time. It's really tough, but at least you're back on your computer now and I'm done being grounded as of Friday night! You know, it's been weird starting to be in touch with you, because we didn't like each other for so long, but I just wanted to tell you that I'm glad we're talking to each other. It's hard to find anyone who really understands what I'm trying to do. My friend Tammy used to, but it seems like maybe not so much anymore. And my friend Lenore is a genius, but she isn't really a theatre person. So it's really, really great, Libby (to be totally honest with you), to think that we are friends now. Even though we sometimes compete against each other, we can support each other, too. It seems like my life is just packed with things going crazy these days. It's nice that you and I don't have to be crazy, too!

Lainey

12 YEARS 2 MONTHS 10 DAYS

I just called Lenore to see if today might be an okay day for me to come over to her house to rehearse. But there was no answer and there wasn't even any kind of voice mail. Weird. Maybe it's a Sunday thing with her family or something. I'll have to ask her about that at school tomorrow.

Meanwhile, it's back to me alone in my room. I'm glad to say that I've now got the entire monologue memorized that I'm using at the audition. It's memorized, but it's not in my bones yet.

That's what Madame Ava calls it when you finally get something so TOTALLY memorized that you don't have to spend any time thinking about what word comes next. She says that's when you can actually start "speaking the ideas" instead of just the words. And that's when you end up saying your lines in interesting ways that make you more like the character you're playing instead of just saying them like you—or even worse, like you trying to remember a bunch of words.

So, bottom line is this: I have the words memorized, but now I have to keep saying the monologue out loud over and over until it starts coming out in ideas instead of just words. That's what I'm about to do now—just as soon as I clean up my room enough that the audience wall is clear and I can perform without worrying about tripping on anything!

FROM: StarChamber@yippee.com
TO: LaLaLainey@yippee.com

SUBJECT: A serious plan . . .

So, listen, Lainey . . . I totally agree with you about the friend-ship thing. It makes me really happy, too. And I have a plan to seal the deal—make us BYACIBFFs (Best Young Actresses in Central Indiana Best Friends Forever).

I still need to get my audition outfit. Do you? Well, let's shop TOGETHER! (I also have a very cool article from *Back Stage* magazine—do you get that? It's really interesting and I learn a lot of stuff from it—including some good advice about audition clothes. Anyway, I can show it to you tomorrow when we MEET UP TO SHOP!) I know it's hard for you to get transportation, so I was thinking we could hit that really cute store in Marion, which is only a couple miles from your house. I remember seeing you rode your bike there when we met at the bookstore that day. . . . (Sorry, again.) Anyway, you could ride your bike and I could get a cab. I'm pretty good at saving my allowance so I have a good stash of cash so that won't be a problem. Then we could meet at the store, help each other find the perfect outfit, and be home before anyone knows anything! AND, here's the most awesome part—I can call your school and act like your mom and you can call my school and act like my mom! AWE-SOME!!! Right? LET ME KNOW!!!

Libby

Not exactly what I was expecting in an email from Libby. I'm not quite sure what to do. Truth is, I've never skipped school before. But I don't really want to say that to Libby. I think she's a little wilder than me, and maybe that's something I need to think about. Maybe I should be willing to take more chances for my career.

Even if it does make my stomach feel jumpy.

12 YEARS
2 MONTHS
11 DAYS

I just couldn't do it. I hope Libby doesn't think I'm completely lame. I'm a little disappointed in myself, to tell you the truth. I think I need to work on my risk-taking skills.

Everything feels totally upside down today in every way. Mom is at work. Dad is gone. It's 7:30 A.M. and Chip is watching TV like nothing in the world has changed.

It makes me want to yell at him. He should not be so calm in the middle of so much drama. "So aren't you even the tiniest bit freaked out by the whole Dad's-not-in-the-army-anymore-and-Marty's-suddenly-coming-home business?" I asked him, rapid-machine-gun style. "Doesn't that affect you in any way?"

"I have my room. He has his. It really doesn't change anything," Chip said flatly.

"What does having your own room have to do with anything? *I* have my room, too, but if *I* wasn't here you'd be thrilled!"

"True. But Marty's room is down the hall. We don't have a common wall."

There's something seriously wrong with my brother, but I don't know what it is, and I don't think I'll understand him until I'm a really old grown-up or until he goes through a boatload of therapy—whichever comes first.

"It's time to go to school," I said to him, but he didn't move. "Did you hear me, Chip?"

"Yeah," he said without taking his eyes off the screen.

That's when it occurred to me—nobody will know if I don't go to school.

FROM: StarChamber@yippee.com

TO: LaLaLainey@yippee.com

SUBJECT: re: re: A serious plan . . .

You can take a makeup test, Lainey! PLEASE!!! It would be so much fun. Besides, you don't even have to call my school anymore because I already did. I just used it as an acting exercise and IT WORKED! PLEEEEEEASE!

Libby.

FROM: LaLaLainey@yippee.com
TO: StarChamber@yippee.com

SUBJECT: re: re: re: A serious plan . . .

I was just going to email you to tell you I want to go, Libby.
And then I got your email! Will you still call my school, though?
Because I think they'd recognize my voice no matter what I did.
The number to my school is 765-555-7834.

Lainey

I kind of made up the part about my school recognizing my
voice. There's only so much risk a non–risk taker can take, and
skipping out on a test to go shopping is pretty much the limit for
one day.

FROM: StarChamber@yippee.com
TO: LaLaLainey@yippee.com

SUBJECT: re: re: re: re: A serious plan . . .

DONE! Get on your bike and start riding! See you there! YAAAY!
Libby

I've never done anything like that in my life before! I gotta say, it
was pretty exciting . . . scary, but exciting! Okay, it was definitely
nerve-racking and I'm actually getting more nervous now because

I'm waiting for it all to get messed up somehow and everyone to find out and then—augh! I don't even know!

I'm not very good at being a troubled preteen. Honestly. Even though I disobeyed my parents when I went to Muncie and now I'm confessing to playing hooky, I swear it's not the way I've always been. If you asked anyone before this year, they would have said, *"Lainey's a little too obsessed with show business and talks about it A LOT and can't talk about much else, but still, she is a good girl."*

I don't know if people would still say that. Not only did someone call the school and lie for me, but I took the fifty-three dollars I had promised my parents I would use to open my own savings account and rode my bike to Marion to meet Libby!

I know it sounds really bad, and I honestly hope my parents don't find out, and not just because they'd be angry. I know it would really upset them and make them worry that they had another Marty on their hands. I don't want to upset them anymore but I also have to say—it was really fun to hang out with Libby. She is just really cool. Sometimes I wonder what it would be like to be her.

I actually got to Fair Play (everybody's favorite store) before her. I was waiting outside when a yellow taxi pulled up and Libby got out. She was already dressed perfectly. She had on white jeans that fit perfectly and about three layers of T-shirts that matched and didn't match in exactly the right way, with purple high-tops. And bouncy hair.

I wished I wasn't wearing a big sweatshirt.

"Lainey!" she squealed, and she hugged me. Like, before I even knew what was going on, she hugged me!

"Hey," I said. "Nice plan." I tried to smile casually.

"Right?" she answered. "Let's go in! We don't have any time to waste since we both have to get home before we get caught!"

"This place has the coolest clothes, without a doubt," I said.

"It's okay." Libby smiled. "But I'll show you some great shops in Indianapolis when we go down there!"

We're going to Indianapolis? Libby is a never-ending surprise.

"But this will do for what we need right now," she said.

I headed toward the Basics section because a good audition outfit needs to be "comfortable but fitted" and "fashionable without being fashion." That's what Madame Ava says. "Black always works." She says that, too. I was holding up a pair of black pants and a black sweater to see how they looked together when Libby came up from behind me.

"That would look really good on you," she said, "but remember I told you I was reading some interesting stuff in *Back Stage*?"

"Yeah," I answered.

"I meant to bring it to show to you, but basically it said that a lot of the smarter actresses are wearing really memorable outfits to auditions now instead of that classic look. The idea is that then they don't get forgotten or confused for anyone else."

"But that's not what my teacher recommends," I said, trying hard to be polite and not let Libby think I didn't trust her advice.

"I know." She nodded. "Classics, right? That's how I've always dressed, too. But I think this is a good idea, so I'm going to give it a try."

"So what does that mean? What are you going to wear?"

"See the green pants and big flowered shirt? It's really cute."

"Seems a little cheerful for Anne Frank, Libby."

"I know," she said. "But that's the point, Lainey. You're going against the type in order to really stick out and be remembered. You don't have to do it, but I definitely am."

"You're going to buy that one?" I asked her.

"I'm not sure. I don't think that one would actually fit me. My legs are too scrawny for that cut. But the colors remind me of a polka-dot dress I have that might actually work . . . now that I'm thinking about it."

"I just don't know," I said. "*Fashionable without being fashion. That's what I was taught.*"

"Totally, Lainey. I get it. That's definitely the safe way to go, and if you're more comfortable with that, then you should get those black pants and that sweater. It's really nice. You'll look fine in it."

There's that *safe* word again. And *fine* is not exactly what I'm after. I'd come this far. I was standing in a store in Marion with Libby Chamber in the middle of a school day. I might as well try on the big flowers and green pants.

I took the outfit and handed the black pants and sweater to Libby.

"Yay!" she yipped, and I headed into the dressing room.

TIME OUT!

For those readers who have never been called:

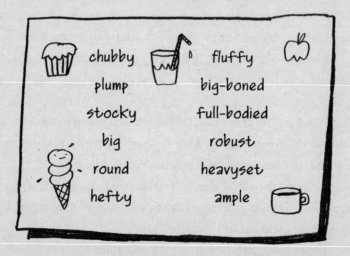

chubby   fluffy

plump   big-boned

stocky   full-bodied

big   robust

round   heavyset

hefty   ample

. . . try to imagine what it's like to try on clothes in a dressing room at a store. You always dread PULLING up, down, or around whatever it is you're trying on. Clothes can look perfectly big on the hanger (and way cute in your head) until you start PULLING. Suddenly, they are ugly, fat-making suits and you don't want *anyone* to see. But your mom is insisting. You say no. Your mom says YES! Then you are standing there while she looks up and down and then shakes her head. That's shopping when you don't weigh what Libby weighs and the worst part? I always think it's going to be different until I'm in the dressing room . . . PULLING!

So imagine how AMAZING it felt when I pulled up those green pants and I didn't have to tug or suck in or anything. THEY FIT PERFECTLY!!!! I L-O-V-E this outfit.

I walked out of the dressing room and waited for Libby to squeal or shout, but instead she just stood there, staring, with her mouth open.

"What?" I laughed.

"That is just SO great on you, Libby. Seriously. It's the best outfit I've ever seen you wear. You HAVE to get this. You will *so* thank me. Please! Tell me you will!"

"It actually fits!" I finally said, because I couldn't *not* say it out loud.

"Oh, yeah!" Libby cheered and put her hand in the air.

"I haven't even checked the prices yet," I said, grabbing for the tags.

"Whatever it costs! I will lend you the money! You MUST have this outfit, Lainey McBride!"

"Pants $19.99 and blouse $24.99—I don't need to borrow a dime!" I announced.

"Let's do it!" Libby declared, and we were off to seal the deal.

I'm home now and, unbelievably, I think I have actually gotten away with everything—playing hooky, going to Marion, spending my savings—all of it! (I hid the new outfit in the back of my closet where it will stay until I get to the audition just to be extra safe.)

I really wanted to call Tammy and tell her everything, but that's not really possible. I did call Lenore to see if we could rehearse at her house tomorrow, though.

"Where were you today?" she asked.

"Oh." For some reason it seemed like a bad idea to confess to everything, so I just said, "Sore throat, but it didn't develop into anything. I'll be at school tomorrow. Do you think we could rehearse at your house after school?"

Lenore didn't answer right away.

"Hello?" I said.

"I'm here," she said. "I'm just not sure tomorrow is going to work. My mother says she needs some space right now. You understand. Maybe we could do it at your house?"

Disappointing. I'm positive rehearsing at her house would be so much better than mine. I've never been to her house, but it must be such an incredibly interesting place, because look at Lenore—how could she not be from an interesting house? Plus, I want to meet her mom. Lenore hasn't said exactly but I think she's an artist, too. (After all, she married one and gave birth to one!) Plus, it's so weird in this house right now that the last thing I want is to have Lenore come here, but I can't think like that. I must keep my focus. I'm lucky to have a seriously artistic person helping me to prepare. That's what I have to remember. Lenore will understand that these living arrangements are not my choice. She will understand that even though my stuff is here, I don't *really* belong here.

12 YEARS 2 MONTHS 12 DAYS

I'm on the bus to school and I have to say, I'm really starting to wonder why nothing has happened after I did what I did yesterday. I mean, I was totally wrong—I snuck around, spent money I wasn't supposed to spend, lied to a friend, skipped school—AND NOTHING IS GOING TO HAPPEN TO ME?! That doesn't seem right. Where's the justice? I mean, I know I should consider myself lucky and all that but nonetheless—my stomach hurts.

I have to stay focused on my audition. I can't let this thing throw me off course. Plus, it's the best way to stay calm. First things first: Find Lenore and square away our rehearsal game plan. I'm sure I'll feel better after that.

I want to say a word about Mr. C. I believe he tried to redeem himself today. He was particularly nice to me this afternoon during my voice lesson, which I think may have been due to one of two things. . . .

1. He felt terrible about his lack of support last week.
2. I was especially good at my voice lesson and he realized he wants to be on my good side as I find my way to fame and fortune.

In support of the second possibility, I did sing well today. I hit every note in "Where Is Love?" from *Oliver*. And, I did it with real feeling. I almost cried real tears. But I held back, because you know what they say about crying onstage:

> *If you cry, your audience won't.*

A good actress can get her audience sobbing simply by holding back her own tears in just the right way.

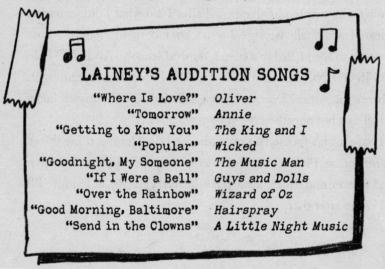

LAINEY'S AUDITION SONGS

"Where Is Love?"	*Oliver*
"Tomorrow"	*Annie*
"Getting to Know You"	*The King and I*
"Popular"	*Wicked*
"Goodnight, My Someone"	*The Music Man*
"If I Were a Bell"	*Guys and Dolls*
"Over the Rainbow"	*Wizard of Oz*
"Good Morning, Baltimore"	*Hairspray*
"Send in the Clowns"	*A Little Night Music*

On another subject, why is Lenore not here? She is supposed to be helping me rehearse right now! I raced home from my voice lesson to be here and she's nowhere to be found. Dad and Marty haven't even arrived yet, so it would be so perfect if she would *just get here*! She's already fifteen minutes late!

There is a whole lot of EVERYBODY in that house, but I just don't think I can face one more thing right now. And even though I've been begging Nana to come for, like, a month now, her car is in the driveway and I'm hiding from her. She must have gotten here after I left for Lenore's house—along with Dad and Marty.

If I had a camera or was a good artist, I would take a picture of me sitting behind the hedge that borders our neighbor's fence so my future biographers (you) could know how awful this moment is.

But not because I want to remember it forever. It's not like that. In fact, I seriously hope I forget all this someday.

That's why I'm doing this. So someone else can be in charge of remembering my childhood and I won't have to.

I guess I've finally been beaten. I'm like the rest of my family now. Maybe I'll just walk through the rest of my life in silence. Maybe this will be the last thing that ever gets written in this archive. But maybe it won't matter because no one will ever come looking for anything that might help them understand who I was as a child because who I end up being as a grown-up won't be interesting enough to make anyone care.

Maybe my dad is right. Maybe all my drama is just drama and the way I see things isn't artistic or special, it's just freaky and selfish. I don't know. I'm so confused.

See, I waited another fifteen minutes from when I mentioned before that Lenore was late and then I decided to just go find her! I guess there was probably a voice in my head telling me this might be a mistake, but I didn't want to listen to it. Probably the same voice that was still making my stomach hurt for not getting caught. Whatever! Lenore was supposed to be here and I wanted to rehearse.

This is what I wanted to happen when I knocked on Lenore's door:

1. Her mom would swing the door open.
2. Her face would light up.
3. She would say, *"Lainey McBride! I am so glad you came. I know I said I needed space but I have been so anxious to meet you because of all the amazing things Lenore has told me about you! Please come in! I'd love to see what you're doing with Anne Frank!"*

But that's not what happened. This is what happened:

I knocked on the door of the house that matched the address inside Lenore's notebook. From the outside, the house didn't look very different from mine. I thought that was really interesting because obviously, on the inside, it would be really different. I was thinking about how interesting it was that such artistic people would choose to live in such a normal house when a man opened the door.

He was wearing dirty sweatpants and a stained T-shirt. He also had a really big stomach and hadn't shaved in a while.

"What's this? The freakin' Girl Scouts?"

I tried to say something, but no sound came out of my mouth.

"Who is it, Petey?" a woman's voice screeched from another room.

"It's the Girl Scouts of America!" the man said, and he laughed.

A woman suddenly appeared. She looked like Lenore but taller and more worn out.

"What is it, honey? Whattya want?"

The woman didn't scare me as much as the man, but I still had trouble finding much of my voice.

"Lenore," I managed to say.

"Lenore?" the woman repeated. "You lookin' for Lenore?"

I nodded.

"Lenore!" the woman shouted. "Lenore, you got someone at the door, but you know I said nobody comes over when you're baby-sittin' and you know we're goin' out!"

As the lady kept shouting down a hallway behind her, I saw the outline of a person appear. The outline started moving toward me. It was holding a baby. It was wearing old jeans and a light green T-shirt.

It was Lenore.

But it wasn't.

She wasn't in black. She had no makeup on. Her shoulders were stooped over, not strong like Lenore's. But that's all I could tell, because she wouldn't take her eyes off the floor. She wouldn't look at me, not even once.

"I'm sorry, honey," the woman said as she turned back to me. "Lenore here knows she don't get company when I'm not home. But I'm real glad you came by. With Lenore bein' new, it'd be good if you'd be friends with her. Not her best quality, I'm afraid, makin' friends. So maybe we'll do this another time soon. Huh?"

"Yeah," I said, finding my voice. "Another time."

That's when I turned and started walking. I kept my feet from running until I was out of sight from the house. Then, I took off and I didn't stop until I got here.

Between the fence and the hedge. A rock and a hard place.

I just don't understand it. I don't understand why she lied to me about everything. It sure doesn't look like her parents are artists to me—at least not her mom.

Also: Who is that baby?

And most of all, who is Lenore?

12 YEARS *2 MONTHS* *13 DAYS*

I'm in my room in bed. Once again, I've proven my fine acting skills. Both Nana and Mom totally fell for my sudden flu-like symptoms:

- Splitting headache
- Occasional sharp gas pains that almost make me double over (almost)*
- *Slight* fever (six seconds with the thermometer near the light bulb)*

So I'm home from school. I know. It's the second time this week and that's sort of a lot of school to miss but it was just plain necessary this morning.

Furthermore, it helped me explain getting home late last night after sitting behind the hedge until it got dark. When I walked in the house finally, just before dinner, I gave Nana a hug.

She said, "Well, thanks for being so excited."

"I'm sorry," I croaked. "I'm not feeling well. I fell asleep at the library and that's why I'm so late. I guess I just passed out."

"You don't feel hot," Mom said as she felt my head.

That's when I pulled out the big guns. I made a tear show up on my cheek.

"My head really hurts," I whimpered. "Can I just go up to bed?"

---

*In all cases, understatement is key.

Nana put her hand under my chin. "You go on," she said. "I'll bring you some dinner in a little bit."

It was so brilliant that I actually felt a little guilty. Nana wasn't mad at me for missing an entire afternoon of her visit. Mom wasn't mad at me for not being here to greet Dad and Marty. And I had the perfect setup for this morning.

FROM: LaLaLainey@yippee.com
TO: StarChamber@yippee.com

SUBJECT: Stylin'!

Hey Libby.

Sorry it's been a few days since I've emailed. Bunch of stuff going on here including that I'm home sick. Plus, I'm feeling a little guilty about sneaking around the other day, but it's not like I wish I didn't do it. It was so totally fun and I LOOOVE my outfit. Thank you so much for helping me find it. I would absolutely have never even seen that outfit if I was at that store by myself. You have a really good sense of style—way better than me. It was really great to hang out . . . even if you are my big competition. Weird, huh?

Lainey

At least I'm catching up on my email while I'm home sick in bed. Bottom line? I just can't face every last thing that is out there today. I had to cut down on some of the stress, and not going to school seemed like the cleanest way to divide and conquer.

Now, I just have to deal with:

1. The return of Marty.
2. Seeing my dad for the first time since finding out the army fired him, which I'm afraid will make him mad FULL TIME

instead of just when something upsets him, which is bad enough considering the way he can bark at every last thing that gets said.

3. Watching my mom melt down every time she sees Marty for the next couple of days.

4. Dealing with the general weirdness that is always there with my family but gets even weirder when there are more of us together.

5. Dodging Nana's stare as she tries to analyze my emotional state from across the room.

What I don't have to deal with is:

1. Lenore
2. Tammy
3. Heidi Almighty
4. The Movie Star Boyfriend Club
5. Mrs. Patchuck
6. Math (this is an accidental bonus)

Oh, and there's one more thing I still have to deal with:

7. My stomachache from not getting caught. (*Really* annoying! I *hate* that I can't be a rebel without feeling seriously guilty. I'm actually sort of wishing I could get caught just to get this over with. But the fact is, the audition is so close now that I just can't risk it, because what if they grounded me so I couldn't go? Okay. I just almost threw up. I have to stop talking about this.)

Nana's been trying to talk to me. I've been polite but even so, I know I'm hurting her feelings by not talking to her but I'm so afraid she'll figure out what I did—she always figures out stuff I don't tell her by the stuff I do tell her—which would be double-bad because with Nana she especially knows my history with Libby. She would absolutely NOT understand what I was doing by becoming friends with her, especially if that means doing things I absolutely know are not the right things to do.

I don't think Nana will even try to understand that it turns out that Libby is the one person who actually totally gets what it is that I feel inside me because she feels it inside her, too. That's why hanging out with her just feels so absolutely great! I feel like I'm in the middle of something more important when I'm with Libby than I do when I'm alone. She makes me really feel like I am who I think I am—someone who's going to do big things! Because I'll be honest with you, sometimes it's hard to keep the faith when nobody around you really understands.

If I told Nana all this, I know what she'd say.

NANA
You should be able to feel special all by yourself. When you start feeling better about who
you are and what you do, then your self-esteem
will improve and you won't need to look for your
self-worth through other people's approval.

Nana has said this to me more than once and I have to say, I don't really understand why. Everybody else in my life thinks I have too much confidence. Nana says, "Methinks she protests too much."

Apparently that's Shakespeare for "if you're shouting about something too loudly, then you're probably trying to convince yourself along with everyone else."

Whatever. Sometimes Nana overthinks things. The fact is, Libby is actually helping me feel better about what I look like and how I behave.

Nana's come up to my room three times already. The first time she brought toast, then soup, and then a *People*. These are the things she said each time:

Toast: "Lainey, are you too sick to do your monologue for me? You could do it without getting out of bed."

Soup: "I bet I could convince your mom to let you come into my room to rest and then we could watch *Access Hollywood*!"

People: "I miss my Lainey."

That last one really stung.

"I'm sorry, Nana," I said as she was turning to leave my room. "I'm handling a lot of things right now—and, of course, being sick doesn't help. I just need some space, I guess, to figure out what's best for me."

Nana was quiet for a minute. Then she sat down on my bed. "I see. Then perhaps you're right to stay up here and keep quiet because if all you're going to do is talk about yourself and what you need, then nobody else really needs to hear what you have to say."

Ouch! *That's* gonna leave a mark.

I told you, didn't I? I knew I should have just kept my mouth shut! Why do I *never* listen to myself? I just hate it when Nana's "sweet grandmother" supply runs out, because she's got a real knack with her "wake-up calls." But here's the kicker:

She was standing at the door to my room with her hand on the knob when she turned back and said, "Your mom had me call the school this morning to let them know you wouldn't be there."

It wasn't until I looked up at her and saw the way she was looking back at me that I realized what she was saying. How stupid! How did I not think about that before I decided to be sick? My mouth opened, but no words came out.

"I understand needing space to sort things out, but I would have thought one day off from school would have been enough. I'm surprised you needed a second one, Lainey."

My face was frozen along with the rest of my body. I seriously couldn't get myself to move. I was totally vibrating with the *thump-thump* of my heartbeat.

Finally, I said, "Are you going to tell my par—"

"Think you might be able to make it downstairs?" she asked, not letting me finish my question. "You have a family who needs you to think about them for a little while."

I nodded and pulled the covers back. I'm not sure if that was Nana's way of saying she's going to keep this between us or if that was Nana's way of saying that she's going to deal with me later, including telling Mom and Dad. Either way, my stomach doesn't feel better yet.

☆ ✳ ☆ 🎭 ☆ ✳ ☆

Marty is here.

It's weird. Really weird. Weirder even than Chip—who, by the way, was so silent tonight, I started to think of his former self as chatty.

Here's how things went when I finally went downstairs:

I waited a minute at the turn in the stairs. If I just lean forward an inch, I can usually see enough of the living room to get an idea of what I'm walking into. Chip was on his stomach on the floor watching old reruns of *Star Trek*. Marty was in the rocking chair behind him. It seemed like he was watching *Star Trek*, too, except his head wasn't quite angled right to be looking at the TV. Maybe he was just sitting there because it was a place to land that was out of the way of anything too emotional.

I could hear Nana talking in the kitchen, so at least Mom was probably in there—maybe Dad. I didn't see him anywhere else. I tried to hear what they were talking about . . . it didn't seem like it had anything to do with me. For the moment, anyway.

I took a deep breath and rounded the corner, slid into the living room and onto the couch.

"Hey, Marty," I said.

He snapped his head around. I guess he was just staring into space, because he absolutely jumped out of his skin when I said his name.

"Hey, Lainey," he said, and he smiled like he was really relieved it was me. "You just appeared, man. How long have you been sitting there?"

"Just now." I smiled back at him.

So, that's how it goes in my family. That's our version of a big welcome-home scene. Oh, except then I said, "Welcome home."

Marty sort of laughed and said, "Yeah, right. Like you mean that . . ."

Okay. I admit it. I didn't really know what to say. It's not that Marty doesn't usually say stuff like that. He's said lots of stuff over the years about how he doesn't belong and how nobody wants him here. But it's usually while he's shouting or slamming doors or heading out the door with a backpack because he's running away. I don't think I've heard him say that kind of thing in a calm, quiet voice. I've always just tried to get away from him before when he was shouting about it. But this way? Calm and quiet? It made my chest kind of hurt and I wondered what it would be like to hug him.

"It is true, Marty," I said, and my voice sounded quiet, too. "It's just extra weird around here these days. But I swear it's true. Mom is totally psyched that you're home. I'm glad you're home."

Then Marty and I both looked at Chip and then back to each other at the same time. Suddenly, I had to cover my mouth so I wouldn't laugh, and Marty looked down at the floor, but I could tell he was biting his lip not to smile.

Because we both had the same idea in our heads at the same time. It was *And as for Chip? Who knows?*

"Well! Look what the cat dragged in!" Nana's voice was like a thunderclap compared to the way Marty and I had been talking. "Glad to see you out and about, Lainey!"

Nana was standing at the doorway of the family room. I was afraid to look her in the eye, so I looked at Mom instead, who was standing right behind her. I only had to glance at her to know exactly what was giving her that funny look on her face.

She was standing in her house and looking at all her children sitting together, and, about to get all emotional again, no doubt. That's when Dad came in from the garage with a big old bucket of tension. Chip spun around and sat up, pulling his legs in tight so he was almost a ball. Marty's shoulders went up about an inch and his eyes dropped down to the floor. Mom hurried back to the kitchen. I could feel myself trying to fit between the cushions on the couch. Only Nana turned and faced Dad without looking nervous.

"Edward," Nana said, "you've got all your kids together here! Isn't that a sight?"

Dad stopped and stared at us. This was not a comfortable moment. It was the first time I'd seen him since the news had come from the army, and it was a little shocking because I swear he looked a teeny bit smaller. He stared at the back of Marty's head and then walked away.

I guess it's just going to be weird around here.

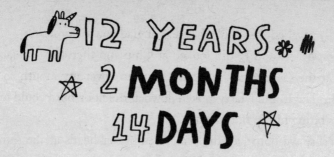

12 YEARS 2 MONTHS 14 DAYS

I didn't, for a second, think about being sick today. I got up and left for school five minutes early.

MOM
You're certainly motivated this morning, Lainey!

NANA
Nothing like a little space to get you up and running again, eh, Lainey?

Nana is really enjoying having my secret in her control. I am really not enjoying it so much. In fact, it made staying home less appealing than another heinous day at Fairmount Middle School. Now, if only it wasn't against the rules to wear hats and sunglasses. The list of people I want to see is as follows:

PEOPLE I WANT TO SEE:
1.
2.
3.

Oh, that's right! How could I forget? I DON'T WANT TO SEE ANYBODY!

Presently, Mrs. Davis is talking about dangling participles and I know, even from here, that this is one of those "I will NEVER need to know this" moments. I will NEVER be at an audition trying to figure out which word in my monologue is the participle that . . . (*which?*) . . . that (I think it's *that*) dangles.

So, instead, I'm taking this time to add the letter I found this morning into the archive.

That's all I'll say.

Dear Lainey,
First of all and most of all, I'm really sorry. I never meant for all this to feel like a lie or to ever seem like I was trying to trick you. The stupid thing is, that's about as opposite to what I was trying to accomplish as it could be. I'll try to explain so at least maybe you'll understand even if you can't forgive me.

You see, Lainey, the Lenore you know from the girls' bathroom is not really me. She's someone I made up a while ago because it felt better to walk around like her than it did to walk around like me. I guess you might say she's Dark Lenore. When I first started at Fairmount I noticed you right away and thought you would be a really interesting person to meet, but you didn't notice me. So when you walked into the bathroom that first time, I couldn't believe it. I couldn't believe you were actually going to eat your lunch where I ate my lunch. I realized this might be my chance to really become your friend, but you didn't actually notice me that day, either. But the next Monday, I came to school as Dark Lenore and, at lunch that day, we talked for the first time. So I just kept being

Dark Lenore and the lies got worse and worse.

Dark Lenore doesn't live with her mom and her mom's boyfriend. Dark Lenore doesn't have a baby brother who doesn't really have a dad. Dark Lenore's mom doesn't clean rooms at the Franklin Hotel (which is how I knew about the Hollywood people, by the way). Dark Lenore hasn't spent the last five years waiting for her own dad to "call her soon."

If you haven't guessed it by now, Regular Lenore is all those things.

Dark Lenore is smart and confident and doesn't care at all if people don't like her. The only thing Dark Lenore and Regular Lenore have in common is this: We both have a dad who calls himself an artist. But the difference is Dark Lenore's dad loves her and makes her a part of his artistic world. Regular Lenore's dad said being an artist made it impossible to be a dad, too.

Oh, and there's another thing that Dark Lenore and Regular Lenore have in common—we both really admire and like Lainey McBride. Lainey is the best friend either of us has ever had and we both feel really, really terrible about lying to her.

So you see, Lainey, I couldn't let you come over to my house, because you would have realized I'm not an artist, I'm not mysterious, and I'm not special. But you found that out anyway.

I won't have lunch in the girls' room anymore and I'm really good at being invisible, so you don't have to worry about bumping into me. Besides, Petey won't last long. Someone new will come along and then we'll move again, because that's what we do.

In some ways, I'm not sorry for what I did, Lainey. Because I really do believe you're amazing and I feel like I learned a lot from you about what it takes to be really different and special and I don't think I would have had that chance if I didn't figure out a way to be different and special myself—even if it wasn't really real.

So just know, I will always remember you and I will always believe in you and if you ever doubt yourself, maybe you can remember how much I believed in you and it will help.

I'm going to see your name up in lights, Lainey. I just know it. And when I do I will be really proud to tell people that I used to have lunch with you sometimes when we were in sixth grade.

Love,
Lenore

I'm starting to think my powers of observation need some serious work, which is more than a little upsetting since an actress needs to really be able to notice things about people's behavior. Madame Ava says that life should be an endless rehearsal. She says an actress is never *not* practicing her craft.

How could I have been so totally fooled by Lenore? How did I not know that Libby and I could actually be good friends? How did I not realize that Tammy really cared more about fitting in than being my friend? Not to mention—I really didn't do too well with putting two and two together to figure out that Marty's school was attached to Dad being in the army and that *everything* (including money) would totally change if Dad got permanently fired from the army.

And how did my whole life get turned upside down in a month?

★ ☆ 😊 🙁 ☆ ★

Nana left a couple hours ago. Now it's just quiet—totally quiet. It's like nobody knows what to say to one another. I think we need a bigger house so we can avoid each other a little better. Nana says we just have to get used to one another again. That's why she left earlier than she'd planned. At least, that's what she said. But I'm afraid it's because she just doesn't want to be around us—me, that is.

We all stood at the front door when she was leaving. She hugged Chip first. He waved. That's his version of PDA. Next she hugged Marty, and Marty hugged back like he didn't want to let go, like he thought it might be the last hug he would ever get. She kissed Dad on the cheek and he said, "We'll talk to you soon, Mom." Then she and Mom hugged and it was the only time it looked like two normal people saying good-bye. The last thing she did was turn to me. She reached out and put her hand on the left side of my chest like she was going to say the pledge of allegiance using my heart.

"Listen to it, Lainey," she said so quietly that I'm not sure anyone else heard.

Then she headed to the driveway and her car. When she started to pull out and my brothers and parents were giving her a last wave, I couldn't stop myself.

Lainey runs out of the house to try and stop
Nana from leaving.

LAINEY

Nana, do you have to go? It feels like we
haven't had any time together.

NANA

That's because we haven't. Next month, don't
spend half my visit sulking. Deal?

LAINEY

I'm sorry, Nana.

NANA

"Sorry" don't pay the piper. Just do better
next time.

Nana raises her eyebrows and gives Lainey a look
as if to ask if she has anything else to say.

LAINEY

Did you tell them?

NANA

Is that really the only question you have for
me, Lainey?

LAINEY

I'm sorry, Nana!

And I couldn't stop them; tears were falling.

LAINEY

I just keep screwing up. It feels like everybody is mad at me no matter where I go. All I
wanted was to get the part of Anne. Why does
that have to make me such a bad person?

NANA

It absolutely doesn't, Lainey. As long as you
don't make your dreams more important than
everyone else's.

Lainey stands in her driveway, crying like an idiot.

                    NANA
    And by the way? You're being foolish about
    Tammy. Make up with her. There are people in
    this world who just know how to accept life
    with grace, Lainey. They make very good friends
    to those of us who aren't quite so good at
    graceful acceptance.

Nana starts the car as Lainey takes it all in.
Then Nana sticks her head out the window one
last time.

                    NANA
    I didn't say anything, Lainey—but not because
    you didn't deserve to be punished. Any more
    trouble and we might revisit this decision of
    mine.

Having Nana disappointed in me? It's new. And I hate it.

It's 4 A.M. and I can't sleep—too much to think about. Maybe Dark Lenore really is Regular Lenore.

I just can't believe that the person I've been having lunch with in the girls' room for the last month is a total fake. Maybe some of the details weren't totally true, but something about Lenore honestly wears black. I just know it.

And she absolutely does know how to say the most amazing things in the most amazing ways. But it almost seems like she doesn't want to be Dark Lenore anymore.

As long as we're talking truths? I wish I could talk to Tammy. I wonder if she misses me. She probably does, because there's no way she could be having as much fun in life with Heidi and Michaela and Susan as she does when we're together. But even if she does, it's really hard to figure out how to find a way back to being friends with Tammy now that so much has happened.

Nana sent me an email when she got home tonight. It said, "Just go to her house and knock on the door. The rest will take care of itself."

FROM: StarChamber@yippee.com
TO: LaLaLainey@yippee.com

SUBJECT: re: Stylin'!

Hey Lainey,

Sorry you were sick. Hope you're feeling better now. This is no time to not be feeling 100%! Are you ready for your audition? Stay cool, calm, and creative! That's what I say. AND DON'T FEEL GUILTY ABOUT FOLLOWING YOUR DREAM!!!!

xo Libby

P.S. Have you rehearsed in your outfit yet? I did in mine. The polka dots are FAB!

12 YEARS 2 MONTHS 15 DAYS

!!!!!!!!AAUUGGHH!!!!!! DISASTER!!!!!!!!!

Three days to my audition and Marty is already in trouble at school!

You may not see how those things are related, but unfortunately for me, they are.

Apparently when you borrow a fellow student's raincoat and then write words on the back of it that I'm not even allowed to know . . . much less say . . . it is enough to get you suspended and make your mom and dad have to go to the school TOGETHER with the other student's parents and meet with your teacher and principal.

You get ONE GUESS when that meeting is scheduled.

Correct! Monday afternoon at 4 P.M.! EXACTLY when Mom should be arriving with me in Kokomo for the audition.

MARTY!!!!! WHY DO YOU DO THESE THINGS?!?!

I knew life was going to be harder when Marty came home. I just didn't realize it would be ruined altogether. I don't want to not be glad he's home. Especially since he already feels like nobody wants him here. But, MARTY! Wake up!

Yeah. I see the irony. Thank you, Nana.

I really want to talk to Tammy. She will help me figure out what to do. I have to find a way to get there!

Here's what I just did.

I walked all the way over to Tammy's house. I practiced my apology speech all the way there. But when I actually got to her porch, it got way harder to get my legs to walk to the door, and so I ended up just sitting down. I know. Weird, right?

Thankfully, Nana is right about Tammy. She is a better person than I am, and when she saw me sitting there, all pathetic and confused, she opened the front door, came out, and sat down next to me. She didn't say anything. She just sat there.

I think she will always be my best friend.

When we finally did start talking, it was like we had never stopped talking. There were so many things to say. Here are some of them:

"I'm really sorry I was so mean about you not standing up to Heidi."

"I'm really sorry I didn't stand up to Heidi."

"I'm really sorry I didn't think about Todd getting in trouble."

"I'm really sorry I haven't helped you get ready for your audition."

"I'm really sorry I said Lenore was more special than you."

"I'm really sorry I couldn't just be happy you had a new friend."

"I'm really sorry I don't really know what's going on in your life and you don't really know what's going on in mine—like Marty is home and my dad isn't in the army anymore."

"I'm really sorry I didn't know all that, and that you don't know that my dad finally left for good."

That one stopped us cold.

"Really for good?" I asked after a minute.

"Uh-huh. He's living somewhere else . . . with someone else."

"Wow."

"Yeah."

"What does it feel like?" I asked her, because that really was the question in my heart. He isn't even my dad and when she just said that it felt like *I* got kicked in the stomach, so I just can't even imagine what it feels like for her.

"Sort of like I don't know what's real and what's not anymore."

We were quiet for a little while, staring down at the ground. When I finally looked up at her, there were tears on her cheeks. I put my arm around her.

"We're real, Tam," I said.

"Good," she said.

And then we just sat there and I didn't tell her about Marty or my audition getting screwed up or how incredibly badly I need to figure out how to get a ride, because right then, Tammy just needed me to help her be sad without being lonely. My heart told me that.

Of course, I'm high and dry on the audition front, but at least my friend feels a little bit better now than she did before I showed up.

☆ 12 YEARS ⚡
✽ 2 MONTHS
16 DAYS ✿

OTHER POSSIBLE IDEAS TO GET
TO KOKOMO ON MONDAY:

1. Skip school, have Mom drive me
   in the morning, and just wait at
   the theatre until audition time
2. Borrow cab money from Libby
3. ~~Get Nana to come back down and~~
   ~~take me~~
4. ~~Ask Tammy to ask Todd~~
5. ~~━━━━━━━~~

PHONE RINGING. Hold on . . .

So that was Tammy.

She is the very best there is or ever will be. No doubt!

She said, "I'm really glad you came over yesterday. I felt a lot better than I've felt since my dad left after we talked about it."

"Really?" I said.

I'll admit it. It feels pretty good to hear that.

"Yup. But I also realized after you left that we did not talk about the audition. You still have two days, right? I can still help you rehearse."

So now I'm trying to check in with my heart to see if it's okay to ask her for help now. I mean, her dad is still gone, but we have to move on to other topics eventually, right? And she did bring it up. So . . .

"Actually, I've got some serious trouble on that front, Tam."

"What?"

I told her all about Mom and Marty and the meeting and the no ride and she just plain shouted at me (really not like her).

"Why didn't you tell me this yesterday?! We have to fix this!"

See, what did I say? The very best. Now and for always.

"I'm hanging up," she said. "I'm calling Cindee. She can get Todd to do A-N-Y-T-H-I-N-G!"

Tammy came over and brought truly THE best news!

"Okay! So! I talked to Cindee, then Cindee talked to Todd, then Todd talked to Cindee, then Cindee talked to me," she said before she even got all the way through the front door.

"Aaaaaand?" I begged.

"TODD WILL DRIVE US TO KOKOMO!"

I swear she said it just like that—in big fat bold letters! So . . . drumroll please . . . THANK-YOU LIST UPDATE: Cindee Binney!

I HAVE A ride to the AUDITION.

Now, as you know, I've been having trouble finding good help in preparing for this audition. I memorized the monologue from the end of the play—the one where Anne talks to Peter about imagining that she's free and walking around in the park looking at flowers. I did that without anyone helping me, and I also rehearsed the monologue about a thousand times in front of my closet mirror. So, I could probably go in tomorrow and give a great audition, but it's *always* better to have a dress rehearsal, because something just happens the first time you do it in front of an audience—even if it's only an audience of one. Like you stand up to start your monologue and forget the first word . . . which is exactly what happened.

Tammy was sitting in the audience chair on the audience side of my room looking at me, and I just stood there—no idea of the first word. Tammy looked at the script.

"Look, Peter—" she whispered.

"I know!" I snapped.

"Sorry," she said. "I thought you were stuck."

All of a sudden I started to get really scared. "I was! I couldn't think of the first line for anything! What if that happens tomorrow? What if—"

"Lainey!" Tammy shouted. "You always forget the first line the first time you show me a monologue. Remember?"

I just looked at her in amazement. She was right. I never noticed that before, because usually the first time I show her a monologue is waaaay before the last day before the audition.

"You'll be okay," she said. "Just do that thing where you shake your whole body, turn around in a circle, and start over."

I nodded and did exactly what she said, and when I opened my mouth, "Look, Peter," came out, and then so did the rest of the monologue. When I got done, I looked at Tammy, who had a huge smile on her face.

"You are sooo going to get this part," she said. "That was good, Lainey. I could really see what you were talking about."

"Thank you for watching it, Tam. You truly are my very best friend, you know."

She smiled just a little bit and nodded. "You too," she said. "What are you going to wear?"

My stomach flipped. Even though we had caught up a lot, there was still so much I hadn't told her yet—like about Libby.

"U-um, I've been trying to keep it a surprise," I stuttered. "It's really different and I want everyone to see it all at once."

"Seriously?" Tammy said. "You're not going to show me? Your *very* best friend?"

I didn't want her to get upset just when we were finally getting back together.

"Okay," I gave in. "But just a peek. I'm not going to put it on. I feel superstitious about it, you know?"

She smiled and nodded. But when I pulled out an edge of the pants and a sleeve of the shirt, she stopped smiling.

"For Anne Frank?" she said. She looked really confused.

"It's a totally different approach that actresses in New York use all the time."

"Really?" she said. "Where did you hear that?"

There was no point in hiding it anymore. She was going to see what good friends Libby and I have become. I might as well start preparing her.

"From Libby, actually. I know it's hard to believe but we really have started to be friends."

The look on Tammy's face was hard to figure out. Sort of like in a scary movie when the actress sees something and she can't tell what it is but she knows it's scary? That kind of look.

"It's gonna be brilliant," I said, and I shoved the piece of fabric back into the closet. "Trust me!"

"I do trust you," she said. "It's Libby I'm not so sure about."

SHOCKER ALERT: Mom came home with flowers for me. I said, "Thanks, Mom!" But she said, "Read the card, Lainey. They're not from me."

Fair Flowers
Good luck!

Break a leg, Lainey! I really
do believe in you.
                    Lenore

27 Main Street   Fairmount, IN

12 YEARS 2 MONTHS 18 DAYS

LONGEST DAY ON THE PLANET. I swear today school started seventeen years ago. But now, the moment has come. Tammy and I are waiting at the curb in front of school for Todd and Cindee. I'm eating Skittles. I wish being nervous made me not want to eat. No such luck.

I also wish my mom were taking me. Don't get me wrong. I'm totally grateful to Todd and Cindee and Tammy, but I'm really nervous and I miss my mom.

When I was leaving for school this morning, Mom called my name after I was halfway down the driveway. I turned back. She was holding out her arms and had a big smile on her face. I ran back to hug her.

"You are an amazing girl, Lainey McBride. I'm very proud of you and I would be there if I could. You know that, right?"

I got a big lump in my throat. I had to clamp my mouth shut to keep it all from showing. I just nodded and then I tried to turn the lump into a laugh before running for the bus. Anyway. She can't be here, so that's that! YIKES! There's Todd and Cindee!

3:25 P.M.

We're in the car. Tammy and I are in the back. Todd and Cindee are in the front. Kokomo is thirty miles away. The audition starts at 4:00 P.M. Yikes, again.

4:03 P.M.

I just signed in and I'm number thirty-seven! *Everybody* wants to be in this show! So far, there are nine girls here for Anne, but there will be more. I mean, Libby's not even here yet. I have to go change into my outfit.

4:09 P.M.

"Lainey?" Tammy is waiting for me to come out of this stall. I'm in my VERY non-classic outfit—really hoping this was the right choice.

"Hold on, Tam, I'm almost ready."

Okay. Enough of this doubting stuff. I look great. I'm going to go out there and rock the house!

4:11 P.M.

Tammy doesn't like the outfit.

"Wow, Lainey." That's what she said when I came out of the stall.

"It's great, right?! It actually fits!"

"It's an eye-catcher!" she said without looking me in the eye.

I feel like everybody is staring at me, and not for good reasons. I wish Libby would get here so that it would become clear that this is what the best actresses do.

I'm sitting in the third row, right on the aisle. Tammy is sitting in the back where friends and family sit. I think Todd and Cindee are sitting with her, but they might be back in the car making out. I really don't know. All I do know is I want to stop thinking about my outfit and start focusing on my audition, but every time I look at someone I can tell they're only looking at my clothes.

Despite the clothes thing, I can still feel that thing that only happens when I'm in a theatre like this. My whole body is vibrating. I get this really full feeling. I love the way everything looks. I love seeing a naked stage with the big brick back wall that's usually hidden by scenery. I love the way it smells, even though I know it's mostly because everything is old and musty, but somehow, this smell comes up out of the belly of the theatre and there's nothing else like it.

OH!! I CAN'T STAND IT! I JUST LOVE IT SOOOO MUCH! IT'S WHAT I WANT TO DO EVERY SINGLE SOLITARY DAY OF MY LIFE.

I want to have a life that lets me go to the theatre every day to rehearse for whatever show is coming up next. I want the people who work at the theatre to know me like they know their families. I want to have a cup of tea in one hand and a script in the other and be carrying a big bag when I pull open the stage door. I want to be wearing a hat and sunglasses. I want to wear clothes that are a total mismatch of all different outfits but somehow, because I'm an actress, I still look cool.

4:15 P.M.

Rodney Vaccaro is talking to everyone right now, explaining how the audition will go. I STILL have not seen Libby. I can't imagine where she is!

"We will spend the first part of the audition hearing everyone's monologues." That's what Rodney V. is saying. He's really nice. I swear he smiled at me like he remembered meeting me!

"Don't worry if we don't allow you to finish your monologue. It doesn't necessarily mean anything negative. We have a lot of people here today, and that's great, but it means we need to keep things moving!"

I know that's what he just said, but we all know that's not really true! If I don't get to do my whole monologue, I think I'll die!

"Right before we break for dinner we will let you know if we need to see you back at seven P.M. for scene work. We will go no later than nine P.M. That's a promise! Okay, everybody? Make sense?"

Puke. Think I might. If I don't get asked to stay for 7 P.M., I will die twice!

Where is Libby?!?!

4:25 P.M.

I don't even know what to say right now. I'm shaking all over and I'm just trying really, really hard not to run out of the theatre.

The Monitor called for Libby Chamber and I was standing up to tell her that Libby isn't here yet when suddenly Libby walked out from backstage <u>WEARING ALL BLACK</u> WITH HER HAIR DYED BROWN!

I'm writing this right now so that I don't have to look up because if I look up, I know I will start crying. DON'T CRY. DON'T CRY! DON'T CRY!

I'm sure Tammy is willing me to turn around right now so she can look at me like, "What's going on!?!" But I can't turn around. Because I don't know. I really don't get it! Why is she not wearing her dress? Oh, please make this not be happening.

Okay. I just looked up.

She looks *just like* Anne Frank!

I feel dizzy.

4:29 P.M.

I wish you could hear the applause right now. Libby just finished her monologue—*my* monologue. As if this isn't all bad enough, we picked the same monologue. The second she finished, the clapping was that kind that explodes and then goes on longer than you think it will. And she just stood there smiling and tucking her *dark* hair behind her ear as if she never expected anyone to notice her.

I can't look at her. I feel so stupid. How did she fool me so completely? I guess she's a better actress than I ever realized. Everything she did, everything she said—it was all just so I would come to the audition looking ridiculous and less prepared than her. It all just fit into her plan.

How am I going to stand up there now in these big flowers and bright green pants?

4:47 P.M.

The Monitor just called my name! I have to put all this away and just get up there and be Anne Frank. I can do this.

4:51 P.M.

My cheeks are burning. I just want to disappear. I forgot a line. How could I forget a line? I was right in the middle of it and it felt so good. I felt like I belonged up there and then all of a sudden, I didn't know where I was. I remember saying "You can have—" and then, I had no idea what I was supposed to say next. It was like I had to come back down to earth to figure out what was going on.

"Roses and violets," someone said. I turned toward the voice and it was Mr. Vaccaro. He was leaning forward and looking at me with a really kind face.

I stared at him and then I started speaking again. "You can have roses and violets . . ."

But I wasn't in the magic place anymore. Now I was feeling my stupid clothes on my skin. I was hearing my heart pound in my ears and I was seeing everyone stare at me like I was the big blond girl in a wacky stupid outfit trying to pretend like she was Anne Frank.

I really would get up and walk out right now, because there's no point in staying, but I can't stand the idea of everybody staring at me in this outfit one more time.

6:00 P.M.

"I want to thank you all for your great courage, patience, and generosity," Rodney Vaccaro is talking to everyone again. "I am truly amazed at how much wonderful work we all saw this afternoon. Please give yourselves a round of applause, because you deserve it."

I'm pretending to clap because I don't want anyone to think I'm not generous, but I know, for a fact, this round of applause is not for me.

"As I told you, we're going to do some scene work at seven P.M. So, if you hear your name, please be back here by six forty-five P.M. so we're ready to go. If you don't hear your name, thank you very much for being here. We will be announcing the cast by the end of the week."

6:19 P.M.

Here is where I am: Subway.

Here is what I am doing: Eating a turkey sandwich.

Here is why: MY NAME GOT CALLED!!!!!

I cannot explain it—have NOOOO idea how it happened. But it did. ANNND, furthermore, only three girls got called for Anne—three, out of *thirty-seven*—me, a girl named Susan . . . and, of course, Libby Chamber.

Tammy is sitting next to me. She hasn't said a thing about Libby, just about how proud she is that I got called for this evening. I guess that's the "grace" thing that Nana talked about.

I saw Libby as we were leaving the theatre. She waved at me! She actually waved at me like she thinks I still think she's my friend. Of course, by the time I made it over to where she was standing by the doorway so I could tell her what I *really* think, she was gone.

Once a snake, always a snake.

6:50 P.M.

I'm back in my seat at the theatre and here's what happened five minutes ago in the girls' bathroom:

"Lainey!" I spun around. It was Libby. "We both made it to scene work! Isn't that great?!"

Stunning, right? You gotta admit, she's amazing the way she just keeps up the act. But I am not fooled!

"Don't pretend like we're friends, Libby. You did everything you could to mess me up. You got me to wear this stupid outfit so I'd look like an idiot and you'd look just like Anne Frank with all your classic black and dark hair!"

The look she gave me? You would have thought I kicked her dog.

"Lainey, you're wrong! I totally put on that dress this morning, but then my little brother opened up the ketchup and it squirted all over me. I had no choice. I had to go back to my regular old boring classic outfit."

"But you're wearing the exact outfit I was about to buy at Fair Play."

"I know it looks just like it, but it's not, Lainey. Truly. Besides, you got yourself all the way here—you made it to the scenework—so what makes you think your outfit didn't help you?"

She's IMPOSSIBLE! I swear she tried to trick me, but on the other hand, like she said, here I am. I don't even want to talk about it anymore.

8:17 P.M.

Rodney Vaccaro keeps putting me in scene after scene! It has all been A-M-A-Z-I-N-G! Here's what he said to me when I first went up to read a scene with a boy named Craig who was reading Peter: "You looked a little surprised when I called your name, Lainey."

I hate blushing. I can feel it when it starts and there's nothing I can do to stop it. I was totally blushing.

"Well, I did mess up my monologue," I said kind of quietly.

"But do you know why you forgot the line? Because I do."

I just stared at him. I really didn't have a clue.

"You were in the moment, Lainey." He spoke really quietly, like this was a private conversation. He was looking right into my eyes like he thought I was really smart and interesting. I could feel people watching us. I knew they were wondering what he was saying, but he was only talking to me. "You were Anne and you were in that attic talking to Peter. We all felt it because you took us there. But then you caught yourself, and sometimes when you're young and haven't had a lot of experience, that feeling can actually throw you off because it really is like being in a different world. Do you understand, Lainey?"

I nodded because I did. I mean, I do. I do know what he means and that *is* what happened and it doesn't mean I'm a bad actress, it actually means I'm a good actress. I just need more experience.

After that moment, everything was like a dream. I read three different scenes with three different people. I even read a scene as Margot, Anne's older sister.

I can honestly say I didn't even notice how Libby did, because I felt so good about how I did. Okay. I noticed a little. She did . . . really well . . . but I'm not thinking about that. My moment. My audition.

8:39 P.M.

Rodney Vaccaro just said, "Thank you, Lainey. That was really lovely. I'm so glad you auditioned. Do you have any conflicts?"

That's a huge question because it's what they ask when you're *really* being considered. It means "Do you have any scheduling conflicts with rehearsal and performance dates."

I said, "Absolutely NOT!"

9:07 P.M.

We're in the car. It went REALLY well.

There was an older actress who was auditioning for Mrs. van Daan who sat behind me for the whole audition. When I got up to leave, she touched my arm. I looked down and she said, "You have a gift, young lady, you have a gift." It made me more sure than ever that I do belong in the theatre.

⬤ ⬤ ⬤

FROM: LaLaLainey@yippee.com

TO: NanaFofana@ditty.com

SUBJECT: The Audition

Dear Nana,

All that's left is the waiting! It was great! I mean, it didn't start out so great but who cares? In the end, it was G-R-E-A-T!!! I really think I did well at the audition and everyone else thought so, too. I know you're not supposed to say anything after an audition, but I *really* think I nailed it and I wouldn't be at all surprised if you'll have to schedule an extra trip down in a couple months to be here for MY OPENING NIGHT!!!

Love,

Lainey

P.S. I think I figured something out. I think why I feel so good when I'm in the theatre is because it's the one place where I can always hear what my heart is saying.

FROM: NanaFofana@ditty.com
TO: LaLaLainey@yippee.com

SUBJECT: re: The Audition

Dear Lainey,

You Shine.

Love,
Nana

It's midnight. I totally can't sleep. I keep playing the scenes from today over and over in my head—especially the good ones—where I'm all alone, in that light, speaking those words while everything else is absolute silence. It's so amazing. I just want to feel it again and again.

I also realized that one of the scenes I've replayed the most, I didn't even mention in my earlier report. I think that's maybe because I don't really know what to say about it. Unusual for me, I know.

Here's the thing—Mr. Mankewicz was there today.

The cranky old man from The Play's the Thing was sitting all the way over in the corner in the very last row of the theatre. I think he must have been sitting there all day, even though I only saw him at the very end. I don't think most everybody else even noticed him, and I'm not sure why I did. But I did.

We were all about to leave the theatre. Todd and Cindee had already gone to get the car and Tammy was waiting in the lobby. I had walked to the back of the house and just turned around to take one last look at everything.

I guess that's why I saw him. I guess I do know. It's because I was trying to memorize the day. I wanted to make sure I had looked at every inch of the theatre before I left so that I would always remember how great it all felt.

When I looked all the way down to the end of the last row of seats, I saw someone looking at me. We stared at each other for a minute and I don't know when exactly I figured it out, but I finally said, "Mr. Mankewicz?"

He didn't say anything back. He didn't even nod. He just looked back at the stage. He obviously didn't want to talk to me but I couldn't help myself, I had to go talk to him.

"Are you auditioning?" I asked him.

"I don't do that anymore," he said. His voice was kind of gravelly.

"But why not? There are actually a lot of parts you could play in this show. I didn't think of it before, when I was in your store. Do you even remember me from when I came in and bought a script?"

"I remember you. You're the perky Anne Frank."

I have to admit it. He kind of hurt my feelings with that one. I think I was feeling so good about my audition that I wasn't ready for him to say something kind of mean. Anyway, before I could decide if I should say anything back to him, he said something else.

"I don't audition anymore, but I always come and watch. It helps me remember why I left the theatre. All this talent and most of it will be sitting at home on opening night. Take you, for example."

My heart started to pound because I was pretty sure he just said he didn't think I'd get the part. I was about to say good-bye to him so I could get away before he said anything else depressing, but he stopped me.

"You impressed me, girl. You really have that thing, don't you?"

He finally looked at me and I couldn't figure out what to say.

"Yeah. You do. I saw it. You're a real-life born actress. But that won't necessarily be enough. That's the truth of it."

"If I stick with it," I said, because I couldn't let him defeat me, "I might get kicked around, but if I stick with it, there's no way a real-life born actress won't end up making it."

Mr. Mankewicz turned back to look at the stage. His head started to nod. "You think so?" he asked.

"I know so," I answered.

"That's because you're eleven," he said, back to his nasty self.

"I'm not eleven. I'm twelve."

He looked back at me and the nasty had turned sad again.

"Break a leg, Lainey McBride."

Then he got up and slipped out a side door I didn't even know existed while I just stood there staring at the empty chair where he'd been.

I really didn't think he even knew my name. But then I realized he probably heard it about sixteen times just today when I kept getting called up to read different scenes. And you know what else I just realized?

That's the start of getting famous!

I should probably put a star here—one that says, "real-life born actress." But something about Mr. Mankewicz and everything he said makes me too sad to turn any of it into a sign.

12 YEARS 2 MONTHS 19 DAYS

This is torture.

JOURNALIST ALERT

Possible Magazine Topic:

"How Young Lainey
Handled the Pressure
of Show Business"

Just print that headline and show a package of Oreos and sixteen bags of Cheetos. E-M-O-T-I-O-N-A-L E-A-T-I-N-G. That's what they call it in all the magazines. It's a no-no. But what can I do? This is stressful. I've checked the Kokomo Players website about 33,254 times today. Nothing.

The Kokomo Players

Magic from Darkness . . .

The Diary of Anne Frank: Cast Announced

Thank you to everyone who came out to audition for *The Diary of Anne Frank*. We were overwhelmed at the level of quality we saw from so many dedicated theatre enthusiasts during the auditions. We wish we could cast all of you. Unfortunately, theatre is a cruel beast and alas only one actor can play one part at one time. Please remember that casting is just an opinion. It is not a fact. Because you did not get cast this time does not mean you won't get cast next time. So if you do not see your name below, please don't be discouraged. You showed up. You opened yourself up to the glory of theatre. You have already succeeded.

The cast for KP's upcoming production of *The Diary of Anne Frank* is as follows: Libby Chamber (Anne Frank); Michael Page (Otto Frank); Joyce Bean (Edith Frank); Karen Errington (Margot Frank); Kirk Swenk (Mr. van Daan); Earlene Helderman (Mrs. van Daan); Craig Hammerlind (Peter van Daan); Steve Taber (Mr. Dussel); Jean R. Bahle (Miep Gies); and Jim Drummond (Mr. Kraler). Also included in the cast are Tommy Boyer, Bob Pabercz, and Paul Dobie as Nazi Soldiers.

This is my last entry into this archive. There's no point in keeping it if I'm not going to be famous. Good-bye.

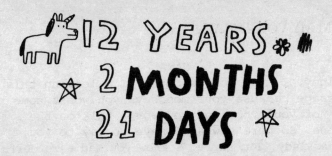

12 YEARS
2 MONTHS
21 DAYS

Okay. I know I said there would be no more entries, but I decided it would be irresponsible as an archivist not to include the following:

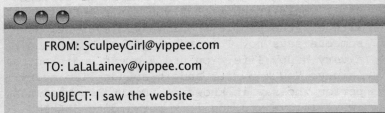

FROM: SculpeyGirl@yippee.com

TO: LaLaLainey@yippee.com

SUBJECT: I saw the website

Dear Lainey,

When you didn't call me back last night, I got worried. Then this morning I realized I could check the Kokomo Players website, so I did. I'm really, really sorry, Lainey! They made a total mistake. I swear it's only because Libby had brown hair. It made her look more like Anne Frank, but as an actress, you were so much better. I really believed you liked that guy who played Peter. The way you looked at him was really, really realistic! Plus, remember that Libby is a snake and did a lot of bad stuff to get where she is. You were amazing. Rodney Vaccaro was really impressed with you and I think something good will come from all this, even if it's not you playing Anne. I am really proud to be your friend, Lainey. Please don't let this upset you for too long. Call me, okay?

Love,

Tammy.

FROM MY VOICE MAIL:

NANA

Lainey, I know you're upset. I'm leaving this message because your mom says you won't come out of your room and you won't talk on the phone. So here's what I have to say to you, young lady. I'm sorry. I know you had a wonderful audition and that you really felt like it might happen for you this time. That is a terrible disappointment. But it didn't, Lainey, and that will be the story more often than not if you are really going to grow up and be an actress. So, I would suggest that you don't cut ties with all the people who love you every time someone says no. That's not going to lead to a very happy life. You had a great audition, Lainey. You know it, and it sounds like every person who saw it knows it. Don't let that slip away! I love you and look forward to HEARING FROM YOU!

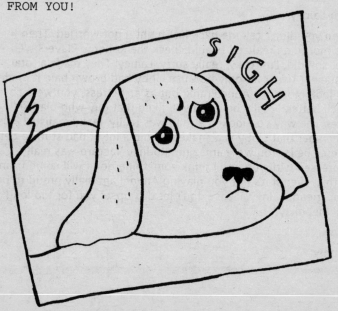

Dear Lainey
The puppy on the other side of this postcard is really sad because you didn't get the part. I'm really sad, too. They will be sorry. I thought you were awesome. Don't give up!
Cindee

LAINEY McBRIDE
2764 OAKWOOD RD.
FAIRMOUNT, IN

FROM: SculpeyGirl@yippee.com
TO: LaLaLainey@yippee.com

SUBJECT: Mad

Dear Lainey,

I am writing to you again because you need to know that you made me feel really bad when you wouldn't talk to me today. I know you are going through a really hard time but that doesn't mean you have the right to treat other people so badly. Lots of people really helped you, Lainey. They're sorry you didn't get the part, too, but they're more sorry that you won't talk to them now. You always talk about how nobody understands how special you are. Well, sometimes I think you don't understand how special everyone else is, too. I'm sorry to be so mean. I hope you will talk to me soon.

Love,

Tammy

12 YEARS 2 MONTHS 22 DAYS

My dad came upstairs and stood at the doorway of my room. He hasn't said anything to me since everything went so wrong. Truthfully, he hasn't said much of anything to me since the night before he left to pick up Marty. This really has not been the best month.

Anyway, he stood where he always stands, just outside my room.

He said, "You know, Lainey, I hate to see you hide up here like this."

I squinted my eyes and hunched up my shoulders. I like to try to get ready when Dad is gonna get mad at me.

Then he said, "You and me don't always understand each other too well and I'm sorry about that, but the thing I've always admired about you is your fight."

I actually felt my mouth drop open. I think it's the first time in my life that my "jaw dropped"—the way you always hear when someone says they were shocked. Mine did. It dropped. To hear him say something so positive? I really didn't know what to say.

"So I hope you don't let this audition business take it from you," he said, and he was looking at the ground.

"You admire me?" I finally said. "My fight, I mean?"

And he said, "Yeah, I do." He stood there for another minute and then he added, "Doesn't mean I know what to do with it though." Then he turned around and left.

Honestly. I'm still stunned. That's about as close to warm and fuzzy as my family is *ever* gonna get!

☆ ☆ ☺ ☹ ☆ ☆

Jaw Drop #2: Marty walked into my room five minutes ago and this is what he said: "Lainey, there's only space for one screwup in this family, and since I'm so good at that job that they won't even let me back in school for a week, you better pull yourself together and get back to being the amazing one."

I didn't say anything because I couldn't figure out what was happening. This talking thing is just not the way my family works. What is going on!?

"I'm sorry if I haven't told you before, but I really am proud that you're my sister. When I was away at school, I used to tell people about how my sister can stand on a stage in front of two hundred people and sing her butt off."

I wanted to ask him if he also told people that I'm an actress, but I knew that wasn't the right response to him finally trying to say something nice to me. So instead, I opened my mouth, but nothing came out. I just couldn't figure out what to say.

"You look like a sick fish when you do that," he said as I stared at him, saying nothing. "Talk or close your mouth."

"Nobody around here thinks I'm amazing," I finally said. "Mom doesn't know what to do about me. Chip can't stand me and Dad is always mad at me—even though, apparently, he admires my fight . . . or something like that."

"You have no idea, Lainey. They don't say anything to you because that's just how they are. But to the rest of the world, they brag about you all the time."

"How do you know?"

"Because *I'm* the rest of the world. There are only three things Mom and Dad ever talk to me about. One, my bad attitude, two, Chip's 'ability to focus,' and three, Lainey's 'talent, determination, and drive.'"

"Wow," I said, because really, it was about all I could think to say.

"Just get back to it. Because without you annoying the crap out of everybody with all your talent and drive, there's way too much focus on my attitude, which really sucks for me."

Then he turned around and left. I believe that sets the record as the longest conversation I've ever had with Marty.

I thought the thing that was hurting me the most was not that I didn't get the part but that I plain old didn't get picked. Not getting picked just hurts. I know I'm supposed to care more about the actual acting than the whole business of "getting picked," but the truth is, not getting picked really hurts (no matter what) and this archive is supposed to be truthful—so there it is.

But that's not the only truth I've decided to tell. It's taken me a while to figure this out, but there's actually something else that's been bugging me even more than not getting picked.

I was lying on my bed cursing Libby's name and wondering why she ALWAYS gets picked AND why she can do so much wrong and not only NOT get in trouble but (amazingly!) get rewarded for it?

How come nothing happened to her for all the tricks she played on me? How can it possibly be that you can do something absolutely wrong and never have to answer for it?

That is when I realized what I had to do to set things right.

I went to find Mom.

I had to sit on the steps for a while before the coast was clear and Mom was alone in the kitchen. Finally, everyone was far enough away that I knew we could have a conversation that would just be between us.

"Mom?" I said from the door of the kitchen.

"Oh!" She nearly jumped out of her skin. "Lainey! How long have you been standing there? I'm so glad you decided to come out of hiding!"

"I have something to tell you," I said, trying to get it out as quickly as possible before I could change my mind.

Mom dried her hands on a towel. "Okay," she said like she wasn't sure she wanted to hear whatever I was about to say.

"Two weeks ago, I skipped school, rode my bike up to Marion, and spent all the money I'd saved to open a bank account on an outfit for my audition."

My guts were shaking. It was like I was frozen and shivering, but I wasn't cold. I could tell Mom was trying hard to figure out the best thing to say. It felt like about four days before she finally spoke.

"Why are you telling me this now?"

"Because you shouldn't be able to do something wrong and get away with it!"

"So you want to get in trouble?" she asked.

I nodded.

"What good would that do? Do you think you'd learn some lesson that you haven't already learned?"

"I just want things to balance out, Mom! I want people who do wrong things to get caught and punished. So I'm starting with myself."

Mom laughed. She actually laughed.

"It's not funny!" I cried. "Why are you laughing at me?"

"I'm sorry, honey," she said. And then she did exactly the opposite of what I was asking her to do. She put her arms around me. "You know, it's not going to make all this fair."

"But Libby did so much wrong! Why doesn't she get caught?"

"You didn't get caught, Lainey. You could have gotten away with your bad behavior if your conscience would have let you. People get away with things. That's the unfortunate truth. And you can't depend on someone else to make sure you do the right thing. It's up to you to listen to the little voice inside you that knows what's right."

"That little voice needs to turn up its volume," I said.

Mom squeezed me tighter. "Or maybe you have to turn down everyone else's and listen a little bit more carefully to your own."

12 YEARS
2 MONTHS
24 DAYS

FROM: LaLaLainey@yippee.com

TO: SculpeyGirl@yippee.com, SmartArt@yippee.com

SUBJECT: PLEASE NOT-JOIN MY UN-CLUB

Dear Tammy and Lenore,

I'm really, really sorry. I haven't been a very good friend to either of you, and I've been confusing my ambition with what I really care about, as my nana would say.

It turns out I haven't been listening to my own voice, and that's gotten me into some trouble that only I can get myself out of—the worst part of that trouble is that I stopped realizing who my REAL friends are. Plus, I've been treating you guys like I hate being treated—not being appreciated for the things that are unique about you.

Tammy, everybody in my family knows you are an amazing person and, of course, it's for the exact reasons that I keep trying to get you to change. So here are the new rules according to me: You shouldn't get mad if you don't want to and you shouldn't speak up if you'd rather be quiet. As my nana says, "You're full of grace and that's a really special thing." You know how to deal with people about all kinds of things without making waves and while making friends. I think it's what makes you such a good spokesperson, among other things. And maybe that's why you can be friends with Heidi, which is what you should be. I, on the other hand, maybe not so much—but that's okay!

Lenore, I wish I hadn't not-noticed you when you first came to

Fairmount. I'm sorry you felt like you had to change who you were to be friends with me. And even though I guess I don't really know exactly who you are, I'm pretty sure that the person I liked so much really is you, and whether you're wearing black or whether your dad is an artist or not—you ARE! You are an artistic soul because look at the character you created! Maybe you pretended when you were trying to impress me, but maybe that was what you had to do to discover who you are. Now you just have to accept who you are . . . just like I do . . . and just like Tammy does . . . and just like everybody does, I guess.

So now for the thing I want to ask both of you: Will you not-join my UN-CLUB? I think if it's an un-club, you probably should not-join in order to be a part of it. Because the whole point of the un-club is to listen to the little voice inside you and figure out what's totally unique about yourself. The un-club will be completely opposite of regular clubs where everyone joins up and tries to be like everyone else. The un-club is about friends helping friends to be their freaky selves and shine as bright as they can!

So whattya say? Will you not-join my un-club and let your freak flag fly?!

Love,

Lainey

12 YEARS 3 MONTHS 1 DAY

FROM: SculpeyGirl@yippee.com

TO: LaLaLainey@yippee.com, SmartArt@yippee.com

SUBJECT: CLIMB

I will totally not-join. But I have an idea about what we should call it—CLIMB.

Here's why: CLIMB is CLUB with the U taken out and I M put in its place.

Because people join clubs to say:

"I want to be exactly like U."

CLIMB is about saying:

"I want to be exactly like I M."

FROM: LaLaLainey@yippee.com

TO: SculpeyGirl@yippee.com, SmartArt@yippee.com

SUBJECT: re: CLIMB

SculpeyGirl, you are a GENIUS!!!!!!!

FROM: SmartArt@yippee.com

TO: LaLaLainey@yippee.com, SculpeyGirl@yippee.com

SUBJECT: re: CLIMB

CLIMB on! Consider me officially not-joined! xxoo ☺

12 YEARS
3 MONTHS
2 DAYS

FROM: LaLaLainey@yippee.com

TO: SculpeyGirl@yippee.com, SmartArt@yippee.com

SUBJECT: re: CLIMB

That is nothing short of Sculpey Genius Squared. LOVE them! Except, can you just tell me honestly . . . does that shirt make me look fat? Ha! Just kiddin' . . . (sort of).

Okay. Enough of this mushy stuff. I love you guys but I have to write to Maeve now. I just read that she's returning to her theatrical roots and doing a big Vegas show . . . AND, she hasn't cast her backup singers yet. Tell me I am not PERFECT for that! Who could be a better backup singer to Maeve Winkley than me? I HAVE to get an audition!

Love,

Lainey

Co-Founder and Non-Member

CLIMB